Single fathers have it rough!
So holds the philosophy of The Daddy Club.

The club is run by men, for men.
The focus: raising children.

A veteran club member will be able to change
a diaper in record time, give a bath without
drowning the child—or himself—and make a
grilled cheese sandwich a gourmet chef would envy.

It's not rocket science, though that might be easier.
It's just about being the best dad a man can be.

Meetings held at Ruth Naomi's Hardware and
Muffin shop alternate Wednesdays, 8:00 p.m.

Please join us!

This month: *Family To Be* by Linda Cajio

Available January: *A Pregnancy and a Proposal*
by Mindy Neff

Available February: *Four Reasons for Fatherhood*
by Muriel Jensen

Dear Reader,

When winter weather keeps you indoors, what better way to pass the time than curling up with Harlequin American Romance? Warm yourself from the inside out with our very special love stories!

There's something appealing about a big, strong man learning to care for a small child, and Linda Cajio's hero in *Family to Be*, the first book in our brand-new miniseries THE DADDY CLUB, is no exception. Ross Steadwell started The Daddy Club to help other single fathers like him—come see what happens when a woman gets in on the fun!

And what's a man to do when the woman of his dreams gets amnesia—and doesn't remember that he's the father of her child? In Charlotte Maclay's *A Daddy for Becky*, Ben Miller has an innovative answer! And up-and-coming author Darlene Scalera is not to be missed with her tale of a million-dollar marriage offer in *Man in a Million*.

Finally, Debbi Rawlins has concocted a whimsical tale of two sisters who trade places for a week and fall in love with men they wouldn't otherwise have met. *His, Hers and Theirs* offers two special heroines, two sexy heroes, two heartwarming love stories—all in one book!

A whole new year is just beginning—start it off right by treating yourself to our four newest American Romance novels!

Happy New Year!

Melissa Jeglinski
Associate Senior Editor

Family To Be

LINDA CAJIO

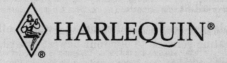

HARLEQUIN®

TORONTO • NEW YORK • LONDON
AMSTERDAM • PARIS • SYDNEY • HAMBURG
STOCKHOLM • ATHENS • TOKYO • MILAN • MADRID
PRAGUE • WARSAW • BUDAPEST • AUCKLAND

ISBN 0-373-16805-5

FAMILY TO BE

This edition published by arrangement with Harlequin Books S.A.

® and TM are trademarks of the publisher. Trademarks indicated with
® are registered in the United States Patent and Trademark Office, the
Canadian Trade Marks Office and in other countries.

Visit us at www.romance.net

Printed in U.S.A.

ABOUT THE AUTHOR

Linda Cajio was always an avid reader who used books as a training ground for her own career. Over fifteen years later, she's still writing romance novels. Married, with two children, Linda claims to keep her sanity firmly rooted in humor. She also claims that writing amid chaos is a constant source of inspiration. She is a graduate of John F. Kennedy High School in Willingboro, NJ, and attended Rutgers University.

Books by Linda Cajio:

HARLEQUIN AMERICAN ROMANCE

*The Holiday Heart

Don't miss any of our special offers. Write to us at the following address for information on our newest releases.

Harlequin Reader Service
U.S.: 3010 Walden Ave., P.O. Box 1325, Buffalo, NY 14269
Canadian: P.O. Box 609, Fort Erie, Ont. L2A 5X3

THE **DADDY** CLUB

Upcoming topics

Week 1:   Diaper Changing for Dummies

Week 2:   Cooking for Kids
              There's life after macaroni
              and cheese!

Week 3:   How To Survive Puberty
              ...Your Kid's!

Week 4:   "Dad" Not "Dead"
              You are *still* a man...with
              certain needs

Be there...
for information vital to every single father!

Prologue

Hardware and Muffins

"I don't think this is the membership I had in mind."

Ross Steadwell surveyed the empty seats before him and ran his hand through his hair, thoroughly discouraged at the lack of turnout. Well, the seats weren't quite empty. His son, Jimmy, stood on one chair, despite being halfheartedly swatted on the butt by his grandmother in her attempt to show the boy the proper body part to match the seat of the chair. Little Ariel, three years to Jimmy's five, sat on another chair, her thumb in her mouth and her eyes solemnly on her father's face. But they were the only attendees at the first meeting of The Daddy Club, a series of workshops for fathers Ross had devised, on everything from diaper changing to surviving a birthday party for rowdy kindergarteners. The club philosophy was If a Mom Can Do It, So Can We.

Maybe the club philosophy ought to be Forget This, Pal.

Ross's mother, Ruth Naomi, made a face at him, clearly reading his thoughts. "So it's not a packed house. These things take time. Want a cookie, honey?"

"No, I do not want a cookie," Ross said, making a chopping motion toward the coffee bar at the back of his mother's hardware store. Ruth Naomi, in a moment of inspired insanity, had installed the eatery in the back half of the hardware store she had run with Ross's father for many years before the elder Steadwell died. She'd renamed the store Hardware and Muffins, and had been instrumental in turning the failing business into *the* place to be. For good measure Ross added, "And no, Jimmy and Ariel do not want a cookie, either. Neither one ate their vegetables at dinner."

"Well, you make that broccoli crap. Nobody likes it but you," his mother retorted.

"They need their deep greens, and, Mom, language."

His mother stared at him for a full ten seconds. Her more-salt-than-pepper hair nearly bristled at the reprimand. "I have language, thank you very much, so your point would be...?"

"Damn!" Jimmy exclaimed.

"I rest my case," Ross replied, returning his mother's death stare. One could be intimidated by Ruth N. or one could be worse than she on the subject. Ross preferred the latter with his mother, mainly because she scared the heck out of him most of the time. Lion tamers knew to never show fear. So did Ross. He'd get eaten alive if he did.

"James Steadwell, if you say that word again, no playing hardware helper for a week," Ruth Naomi admonished Jimmy. "And if I say it again, then no playing hardware helper for me. Okay?"

Jimmy frowned. Hardware helper was his favorite game. "Okay. I'll help you speak nice, Grandma."

"Okay," Ariel added for good measure, after popping her thumb from her mouth. "Can I have a cookie now?"

"Sure," Ruth N. replied, smiling happily.

Ross rubbed his face in frustration as his mother led the children away from the meeting space. The *empty* meeting space. His Daddy Club was an abject failure before it had even begun. Not a single male had shown up for the organizational meeting. Not a single male in Princeton, New Jersey—and the town was loaded with divorced dads—was willing to admit he needed parenting help. His mother, veteran instructor of her store's Hardware for Women Koffee Klatch, had no problems filling her twenty-seat meeting space with females who needed or wanted to learn home improvement. She had suggested he do the same with a Daddies' club, after Ross had come through almost two years as a widowed, single parent.

"Here's a macadamia nut, chocolate chip muffin," Ruth said, materializing next to him with said muffin in hand.

"Nice of you to listen to me." Ross accepted it anyway, and took a bite. The sweet, crumbly texture was enhanced by the melting chocolate chips and rich nutmeat. "You know you're a rotten mom giving me food for comfort. All the child psychologists say so."

His mother looked around the store. Seeing her grandchildren occupied with Margie, who ran the coffee bar, Ruth Naomi told her son exactly what the child psychologists could do to themselves.

Ross chuckled. "That's what I like about you, Mom. You tell it like it is whether I want to hear it or not."

"Listen, you deserve a little 'feel-good,' my angel." She put her arm around his shoulders and gave him a hug. That she was six inches shorter than he didn't deter her from yanking him down to her level and planting a buss of affection on his cheek. "So nobody showed up. So what? They'll come. My first workshop for women was attended only by you and Barbara, if I remember rightly."

"You do." Ross smiled a little at the mention of his wife. Barbara, who thought Ross couldn't find a spoon in a kitchen drawer, would be amazed at how he'd coped after her death almost two years ago. In fact, in learning to cope with two very young children, a fast-paced job as a computer salesman and the loneliness, he had felt the need to talk with his fellow men on how to do everyday kid and household things. His mother, sensing a good promotional move for her store, urged him to give workshops for men on being moms. He couldn't believe he'd actually bought into it.

"I'll get the flyers out for next month," Ruth Naomi said, breaking into his thoughts. "Guys will turn up. You'll see."

"Forget it, Mom." Ross shook his head and took another bite of the muffin. "Can I have this recipe?"

"No. You *will* do this."

Ross walked away. "Kids, come on. We're going home."

"No, no!" Jimmy and Ariel whined, even though both had had full days.

"If you hold it, they will come," Ruth Naomi intoned.

Ross turned around. "Mom, this isn't flipping *Field of Dreams!* It was a noble experiment that failed."

"One more time, just one," Ruth wheedled.

"No."

"Don't disappoint me, son," Ruth said, bringing out the big guns.

"I hate it when you do this," Ross muttered, taking his children by the hand and leading them toward the door.

He could say no all he wanted, but he knew he'd try one more time. The Daddy Club *was* a good idea.

And like his mother, he hated to be wrong.

Chapter One

He *was* everything his voice promised.

Elaine Baransky gaped at Ross Steadwell as he came through her office door. Tall, slim-hipped, with dark hair and piercing blue eyes, Ross had a face of planes and angles that sorted themselves out in a pleasing symmetry. Very pleasing.

She had only spoken to him on the telephone previously after months of needling by her assistant, Tina. Tina had never met him, but true to Tina's promise, his voice had been whisky over gravel. Kris Kristofferson, John Cusack and Robert Redford combined couldn't have sent the shivers down her spine the way Ross's voice had. His company, RP Computers, wasn't one with whom her company, Data, Ink, did business. Not that it was supposed to matter. He looked downright hot.

The two kids who came through the door behind him didn't.

The little boy was sullen and the toddler girl with Ross's blue eyes had her thumb in her mouth. Tina looked on as she held the door open, her expression a mixture of amusement and horror.

Elaine stared from Tina to the kids, knowing her

mouth was agape. Never had anyone brought children to a business meeting.

The boy looked at Elaine, then announced, "I wanna go home, Dad."

Elaine wasn't surprised by the reaction. Young ones normally didn't respond well to her which was one of the reasons she didn't have children of her own.

Ross Steadwell thrust a bag into the boy's hands. "Play Indy 500, Jimmy, and be patient. You know what I said."

Jimmy dropped to his knees on the spot and began pulling toy cars out of the bag to race over Elaine's Aubusson carpet.

Ross turned to Elaine, smiling hopefully at her. "Let me be the first to say that I can't believe I'm doing this, but have you ever been backed to a wall, Elaine?"

The deep, smooth-rough voice poured over her like a fifth of Jack Daniel's at a Tennessee bar. The heat of it spread down to her toes, even more powerful now that it wasn't muted by the telephone lines. She wanted to drop to her knees on the spot, because her legs wouldn't hold her up much longer.

"Have you ever planned and prepared for a meeting only to have disaster strike at the last moment?" Ross continued. "In order to keep this appointment with you, I'm forced to bring my children because my baby-sitters and backups fell through." He muttered a cryptic "They all had to eat the cannoli, dammit" before adding, "I apologize profusely and promise Jimmy and Ariel will not write on your walls or break your vase—" He looked around while she was still speechless. "You don't have any vases. Good move on your part. They won't break that modern sculpture, either, since it's made of bronze. It *is* made of bronze?"

"Yes," Elaine finally croaked out, horrified by the first impression her voice made.

She still reeled from the obvious reality that this man from RP Computers, who had worked his way in through six months of friendly phone calls and scads of trade literature, had brought his children to a meeting. She forced herself to voice the other obvious reality. "Mr. Steadwell—"

"Ross."

"Ross." Oddly, the name felt at home on her tongue, distracting her from her purpose. That disturbed her almost as much as the two children did. He'd had such a sexy voice on the telephone, but this...this was not the business meeting she'd been anticipating.

"Vroom, Vroom!" Jimmy shouted happily, whipping two cars over the rug's plush pile.

"I don't think this will work," Elaine said lamely, as she gazed at Ross's intent blue eyes.

"It *will* work," he insisted. "Just as I will work to make the best deal for your company. Jimmy, easy on the starting gate, boy, while I talk to the lady."

That wouldn't be enough, Elaine thought, thoroughly disheartened at Ross's audacity. She found her gaze shifting to the little girl, Ariel. The child couldn't have been more than three or four, but she had such a solemn stare. Big blue eyes gazed at Elaine, totally captivating her with their directness. Children normally didn't respond to her, but something in the way this one looked at her, as if the child could see through the facade, hypnotized Elaine. The sexy male voice cut across her fog.

"I'm a single father, Elaine, with total responsibility for my children. I normally have baby-sitting backups on backups, but they failed me today. However I want you to know that should Data, Ink, award its new project to RP Computers, I will care for your account as I care for my kids. Twenty-four hours a day, seven days a week. I'll take it with me everywhere I go, nurturing it to perfection. If I don't, you can break any agreement we have right on the spot with no contractual repercussions.''

Elaine dragged her gaze away from the child to the adult. Kids at a meeting! What was he, nuts? ''Mr. Steadwell...Ross...we can't have a meeting—''

''Sure we can.'' He grinned at her. ''Jimmy's settled with his cars, and Ariel's a good little girl. You won't know they're here.''

Elaine took a deep breath, knowing what she had to do. ''Would you bring your children to this meeting if a *man* was the regional manager for Data, Ink, instead of me?''

His good humor vanished and he stared at her with a suddenly very cold, very determined gaze. ''I brought my children only because I had no choice, not because you're a woman and I think you might tolerate it more than a man would. I brought them because having Data, Ink's business is so important to my company that I will let nothing stand in the way of getting it, even if I have to make a major business gaffe like this one on my one chance to see you. Bringing my kids today should show you that I will not ignore your account for any reason. You will be my highest priority.''

Elaine gazed at him a moment longer, yet out of the corner of her eye she saw the little girl wrap her arm around her father's leg for protection. The gesture was touching, as if the child were also protecting her daddy. Elaine knew she shouldn't respond to it. ''That is the biggest load of BS I have heard in a long time. And I'm impressed.''

She must be the biggest idiot on the east coast. Wait until Burt Langdon, head of Data, Ink, heard what she was doing. He probably already had heard, the moment Ross entered the building with two kids and asked for her office.

Ross relaxed and smiled. ''Thanks for giving me a chance.''

Elaine shook her head. ''Don't thank me. You're working with a tremendous black mark that's not going to get better. But because we have a need, I'll hear you out. Come and sit down.''

It was those baby blues, she thought as she returned to her chair. But which ones got to her, she couldn't fathom.

With Jimmy vroom-vrooming fairly quietly behind them, Ross got items out of his briefcase. Or tried to. Ariel sat on his lap, hindering him as he rifled through the case balanced precariously on his free knee.

''Tina gave me specs on your proposed information system.... Here we go.''

He pushed a report of several pages toward her and began to explain what equipment RP Computers would use to bring their database to its most efficient use. Somehow the numbers all blurred together for Elaine as the voice once again worked its magic. She envisioned him talking to her in a more intimate setting, saying much more than numbers and prices. His hands were strong and yet slender, clearly nimble, and she wondered what they would be like skimming over her body.

Elaine realized just how distracted she was and mentally shook herself. It had been a long time since she'd had a relationship—any relationship—with a man. She was twice divorced, her first marriage a mistake in her senior year of college, and her second a mistake of thinking she and George were fast-track executives who would understand the long hours. She now considered herself above the fray of man-woman relationships. Her response to Ross was more sex starved than a teenager with a case of raging hormones.

Ariel slid off her father's lap. She came around the desk and wedged herself between the arm of Elaine's chair and the desk itself. Not knowing what else to do, Elaine backed her chair out to keep Ariel from being squashed. Ariel grinned at her around her thumb. Elaine grinned back.

"Ariel, honey, come back over here," Ross said, interrupting his facts and figures.

"She's okay," Elaine assured him, not wanting an emotional tug-of-war between father and daughter. Ariel wasn't hurting anything, and Elaine, in a mushy moment, thought it was kind of nice to have the child near her. Ariel began toying with the papers on Elaine's desk, not crumpling them, just twisting them back and forth with her free hand.

"Are you sure she's okay?" Ross asked, his silky voice dubious.

"Sure." Elaine wasn't so sure about Jimmy, who was spinning in circles behind his father's chair as he played race car driver.

Ross went back to his pitch. Elaine forced herself to concentrate on the words in black-and-white rather than the voice. She had to admit that Ross Steadwell had done his homework where the database was concerned. Tina had clearly given him a heads-up on what kind of prices to expect from the competition, because Ross was in the ballpark, preliminarily. Little Ariel wedged her butt up against the side of the chair and Elaine's thigh while Elaine was reading the proposal. When the child pushed up on tip-toe, it seemed easy for Elaine to shift and accommodate the kid on the chair with her.

Elaine marked off a few things she questioned on the report. Ariel picked up a pen from the desk and began to draw on a paper in front of her. Elaine watched the child make a big circle around Burt Langdon's latest memo. The man killed whole forests with his three-times-daily memos.

"Ariel, no!" Ross said, reaching for the pen.

"No, it's okay," Elaine countered. "I've already read it."

She didn't add she couldn't think of a better way to recycle than letting Ariel express herself all over the paper.

"Potty," Ariel announced, taking the thumb out of her mouth.

"But we just went before we came in here," Ross exclaimed, clearly exasperated.

Ariel pulled the thumb out of her mouth. "I gotta go potty, Daddy."

"Oh, Lord." Ross laid his forehead down on the edge of Elaine's desk and gently banged it a few times.

"I don't think it works that way," Elaine told him.

Ross raised his head. "I am sorry, Elaine. This has been a total disaster, but I didn't want to lose my only chance at the account. I have, anyway."

"Well, I don't know," Elaine admitted, tapping the report with her pen. Ariel reached out and took it from Elaine while Elaine added, "Actually this initial proposal looks feasible for our needs."

At that moment, Ariel's artistic creativity sought

new horizons. The kid reached for the RP proposal. Elaine and Ross yelped at the same time and grabbed it from the desktop before Ariel could do her thing all over it.

Ariel's features turned down in the classic prelude to tears. "I wanna go potty!"

"Right, right, right." Ross got up.

"No. Her."

Elaine sat up in shock. "What?"

"No, honey," Ross said gently, his voice at its most tenderly persuasive. "Daddy will take you."

"It's the door on the left," Elaine said, pointing to her personal entry to the executive bathroom. Taking the child to the bathroom would be a disaster for her. She wouldn't know what to do first or last, although it was nice of Ariel to think she would.

Ross came over and lifted up his daughter. His hands brushed Elaine's breast accidentally. Her body turned so hot she thought she would pass out from the touch. Obviously his virility wasn't limited to face and voice. Ross seemed oblivious to her response. Elaine thudded back to earth when the bathroom door closed behind Ross and Ariel. She was alone with Jimmy.

"Hi," she said, trying to be friendly.

Jimmy said nothing, just kept spinning around in a circle while he raced his cars.

"Isn't that going to make you sick?" she asked.

Jimmy paused. He looked at her, but said nothing.

"Well, one Steadwell won't get to me," she muttered.

"My grandma threw up," Jimmy suddenly announced.

Elaine blinked. "She did?"

"That's why we hadda come today with my dad.

I'm not allowed to talk with you. Dad said. But my grandma threw up.''

Jimmy went back to his cars.

Elaine realized that the baby-sitter Ross mentioned who had failed him must have been the children's grandmother, whom Jimmy said was ill. She smothered amusement at the thought of how Ross would react to the boy's blunt explanation. The poor man would probably have committed himself at that point. Clearly, he struggled with parenting. She wondered how he became a single father and figured it was probably from divorce. The mother must have walked out or been incapable of caring for the children. Elaine shivered, knowing the latter was her own worst fear about having children. She could barely cook an egg sandwich, let alone care for little ones. Kids didn't like her much, anyway. Ariel was the exception.

Ross emerged from the bathroom with Ariel in hand. He glanced at Jimmy, then glanced at Elaine. ''I have to apologize again for this and tell you it isn't going to work. This meeting, I mean. Ariel just announced she will have to go again in 'a widdle bit.'''

Elaine felt the grin spreading on her face. ''How long's a 'widdle' bit?''

''Anywhere from five minutes to five hours—''

''I gotta go,'' Jimmy said, standing up.

''Or five seconds, if it's her brother.'' Ross pointed to the appropriate room. ''No splashing the water, kid.''

Horrified, Elaine blurted, ''He splashes the water in the—''

''No, no,'' Ross broke in, laughing. ''In the sink.''

After Jimmy disappeared into the other room, Ross sighed loudly. ''Elaine, thank you for giving me time today. And for your understanding. I'd like to explain more but we've been derailed so many times that I don't think we'll get back on track. Trust me. What I'd like to propose is another meeting, this time dinner and a choice of *Rent* or a hockey game. My company has season tickets to both. We can discuss my proposal for Data, Ink, and have a little R&R, too.''

Elaine normally would have been pleased to have a choice in evening business entertainment. Most men didn't ask for her tastes when making arrangements. While many deals were hammered together during a night out, she couldn't help feeling as though this was a date. She mentally shook herself, then weighed the figures he'd gone over briefly against what she knew her company would be looking for. RP Computers wasn't out of the ballpark. She knew she owed it to her company to listen to him further.

Nice justification, her brain told her. Her body, however, loved the idea of being next to him all evening. Cozily next to him. Elaine pushed the thought aside. She was all business. ''All right. Dinner and the game is fine.''

Ross's eyebrows shot up. ''The game? I would have thought— Never mind. I'll get myself in trouble.''

Elaine chuckled as she rose. ''You certainly will.''

She shook hands with him. His grasp was firm, warm and protective even as a current of sensuality ran through her. She let go abruptly and, not quite looking him in the eye, said, ''Thank you for coming in.''

''Thank you for seeing me,'' Ross replied, his voice flowing over her like dark, rich honey.

Elaine realized she'd stopped breathing. She let out her breath and turned to Jimmy, who was happily throwing his cars in a case. ''It was nice meeting you.''

Jimmy looked up, then to his father. "I was good, Dad. Can we get ice cream now?"

"I want ice cream, Daddy," Ariel announced. She smiled at Elaine. "You're pretty."

Elaine warmed to the child. It was hard not to, even for a kid-goof-up like herself. "Thanks. You're pretty, too."

Ariel tilted her head and smiled. "I know that."

Ross looked heavenward. "She's not shy in the ego department. Is Friday evening all right? Hopefully, one of my baby-sitters will be over her illness then."

Definitely date time—only the man was fishing for business not sex. Disgusted with her thoughts, Elaine said, "Friday's fine."

After Ross and his entourage left, Tina shot in the door. "I can't believe he brought his kids!"

"Neither can I," Elaine murmured thoughtfully.

"That killed the voice right there for me, let me tell you," Tina commented, shivering. "So what did you do? Kick him out after slaying him with your tongue?"

Elaine frowned. "Hey! I'm not that bad."

"Right, and that's why Bob Hopplemen is still try-ing to recover from the last meeting with you."

"Bob didn't take care of the Parsons account, and we lost it," Elaine countered. "He's lucky he's not out of a job. But no, I didn't 'slay' Mr. Steadwell. I'm seeing him Friday for dinner and a hockey game, to further discuss the proposal."

Tina's eyebrows shot up.

"Don't say it," Elaine said. "I've got your annual review on my desk."

"Rats! I had something pithy, too."

"Well, pith it on out of here. I've got work."

Dinner and hockey. Elaine wondered if she had the worst case of burnout ever seen.

She burned all right. And how.

"COME ON, REF! There's got to be a penalty there. You have to have a penalty!"

Ross glanced at the woman who leaned out of the open window of the luxury box and shouted down to the hockey match below, adding her voice of protest to the entire arena's. The noise was deafening.

Elaine Baransky had been a surprise. He'd been expecting a woman in her late forties and tough as nails, rather like a younger version of his mother. Instead she was about thirty and femininity at its prime. The fiasco with the kids had distracted him a little from Elaine, but now he had been receiving the full impact of her. She hit hard.

As she glanced over her shoulder at him, her eyes had a sparkle in their brown depths, especially aroused as she was now. Her strawberry-blond hair was left loose and flowing tonight, a wave of shiny tresses caressing her shoulders. Ross itched to run his finger through the strands, to see if they were as silky as they looked. Her snub nose, sprinkle of freckles and the roses in her cheeks made her look almost teenage cute. Her body was even better, willowy with long legs that could deliciously wrap themselves around a man when making love. Her tight derriere tilted up as she leaned over the box sill, offering the sensuous deal maker of the night. She was no tough-as-nails battle-ax.

Ross paused. His libido had been dormant since his wife had passed away, her long illness and the aftermath taking its toll. Maybe that's why Elaine hit him like a shot the moment he'd looked at her. He just needed sex. At least that's what he told himself.

Elaine's gaze blazed with indignation. "Did you see that weasel Popov high-stick McMarter right in the ribs? How could the ref miss that?"

"They hire 'em that way," Ross replied, chuckling at her.

"No kidding." She grinned. "McMarter'll get his revenge. Third period in the last two minutes when the refs really fall asleep on penalties."

"I didn't peg you as a knowledgeable hockey fan," Ross said.

Elaine chuckled. "It's the price of doing business these days. I decided that if I had to go to sports games for the company, I might as well learn what was going on. Now I actually like them."

"A woman after a man's heart," Ross said, appreciating her enthusiasm.

"It's more like a woman in a man's job," she retorted. "But what the heck. My dad says it's nice to talk sports with his kid."

Ross wondered which of his two would be the sports talker. Despite Jimmy's preoccupation with cars, it would probably be Ariel. She always surprised him.

Elaine pushed herself back inside RP Computers' private box and sat down on the sofa. After reaching for her soda, she said, "How long have you worked for RP?"

"About four years," he replied, knowing she was getting down to business. Dinner had been an easy talk of foods and the stock market, something else he had in common with Elaine. He had tried to keep the meal in perspective, but found himself interested on much more than a business level. That disturbed his sensibilities even as it disturbed his body in more intimate ways.

In the course of his job, he had spent evenings alone with the occasional woman manager, all strictly business, a line he had never once thought to cross. The more casual corporate atmosphere was designed to ease awkwardness, to present one's self and one's proposal in a less-pressured manner. That such evenings held a hint of corporate material wealth on the host's part and a little gentle bribery, as well, didn't hurt. However, in the case of Elaine Baransky, the whole thing had the feel of a date.

Mentally he pulled himself together. "The company's been great to work for, very caring. We pride ourselves in giving personal attention to our customers. Management prides itself on giving the same to its employees."

"That's right out of the corporate brochure." Elaine grinned at him.

"Probably," Ross admitted. "But it's true. After my wife died, they told me to work from home and be with my kids before I even had to ask."

A funny expression crossed her face. "Oh, I thought...I'm sorry, I didn't know your wife passed away. That must have been a rough time."

"It was. It happened almost two years ago. She'd been ill for a while."

"I'm sorry."

Ross heard the sympathy in her voice as well as saw it in her expression. He loved Barbara, but marriages were complicated things, and what one expected one didn't necessarily receive. Before her illness, Barbara had been the perfect wife and mother, perfect to the point of becoming more and more rigid and controlling.

Maybe it had been the stress of having two young children and a husband with a demanding job that had caused her growing unhappiness. Maybe a manifestation of the tumor had been her personality change. Ross didn't know. At the end, he and Barbara had come together and that, to him, was the most important thing.

"I'd like to thank you again for your patience with me the other day," he said to Elaine. "That kind of flexibility is rare in our business."

Elaine smiled, although the sympathy faded. "I'm kicking myself that I showed a vulnerable side."

"I hope to take advantage of it."

He had meant the words in the same business sense she did, but somehow their meaning charged the air with something more than business. He stared at Elaine, seated next to him, and felt the sofa suddenly shrink into the dimensions of a child's chair, the two of them seemingly crammed up against each other, near to touching. Out of the corner of his eye, he could see her breasts rise and fall as her breath quickened in response. A telltale flush rose to her skin, that delicate pink hue that said she was aware and aroused. Thank God they were alone, he thought, the early-hockey-season game not attracting other RP reps and their clients. Another month and the place would be packed.

"Ahem." He cleared his throat even as she shifted away from him. "Did you get a chance to look over the proposal I offered?"

"A bit. It needs more work, but you're not out of the ballpark." She wouldn't say too much since she couldn't reveal exactly what another company offered. "Although we have a contract with Dall for much of our hardware, I'd like to get a bid going on this. I like the way your company is flexible with us."

Ross grinned. The words were music to his ears, hard-driving rock music that he'd fallen in love with as a fifteen-year-old. Twenty years later he still loved it. In fact, she was telling him more than just a proposal. Dall Computers had come into the corporate market with hurricane force, offering such dirt-cheap prices that no one else could compete. He'd heard vague rumors that what customers were promised and what they got didn't match up as well as it should. Problems were brewing. If he could ensure service and quality would be top-notch, maybe he would get an in with Data, Ink. The commissions would be tremendous. He could baby-sit their account alone and retire in three years.

"Flexibility is our trademark," Ross said. "See how flexible I was the other day? I juggled kids and proposals at the same time."

Elaine burst into laughter. "I think the kids juggled you. Your daughter certainly juggled me. Kids normally don't like me."

Ross frowned. "My kids did."

"Ariel maybe." Elaine shrugged and rose from the sofa. She walked over to the canapé tray. "I'm not the domestic type. I guess that comes from being an only child. I can barely cook an egg."

"Nobody's that bad," Ross protested.

She made a face. "I am. My mom freezes food every week for me, just so I get homemade meals once in a while. Kids…it's just as well that I'm involved with my job. They're beyond me."

"I think you need my Daddy Club more than I do."

She frowned, shrimp on a cracker paused halfway to her mouth. "What?"

Ross rose from his seat and walked over to her. He

took her wrist and pushed the cracker the rest of the way to her mouth, the act holding a whimsy and a familiarity that troubled him. He quickly pulled his fingers back. Clearing his throat and feeling the nervous gesture betray his emotional state, he said, ''I started, or tried to start, a series of workshops for single fathers on how to keep the laundry from turning pink or how to apply first aid when your kid falls off the ottoman. Just general everyday stuff that men are used to their former wives doing. Only nobody showed up for the first meeting.''

Elaine chewed and swallowed her shrimp and cracker, frowning thoughtfully the entire time. She took a sip of mineral water, then said, ''I can't believe no one showed up for it. *I* would have. If I were a man.''

''But you're not, thank God.''

The words hung out there, like fresh sheets billowing on a warm summer breeze. Ross stared at Elaine, his brain cursing his giveaway statement while his blood turned hot in his veins. She looked so damned good, he thought, with her wide-eyed gaze, curvy form and gamin looks. How the hell would he ever get past that?

Even as he told himself he would never do anything to jeopardize the thread of business connection he'd finally started to put through the needle, he leaned forward and captured her lips with his own. She tasted salty and sweet and a little bit like the sea, all at the same time. He loved the sea. Her mouth was warm and soft, her lips incredibly pliable. Even with the shock she must have had at the first touch of the kiss, she was already responding, adjusting to the pressure of his mouth on hers.

His brain kicked in just as suddenly as it turned off, and he pulled away from her. His breath came in gasps, as if he'd been hit by an 18-wheeler. His body trembled with the shock of what he'd done…and with how damn much he hadn't wanted to stop.

"I apologize," he said, shaking his head ruefully. "I have *never* done that before with a business associate. I don't know how I could have done it this time."

She glanced away from him, then back again, her cheeks bright red. "I…you weren't alone in the kiss…in what happened, I mean. I know I'm not innocent and I won't allow you to take the blame all by yourself. I, too, have *never* done such a thing before with a business associate."

He had to say the words that would kill him, professionally, financially and personally. "I understand if you don't want to hear from me again. But I'm asking you not to hold this against RP Computers. I'll get another sales rep assigned tomorrow."

"I won't hold it against your company or you." A faint flush hadn't quite faded from her features, giving her face a soft pink glow that only enhanced her attractiveness. "How can I, when I'm just as guilty?" She smiled slightly. "However, I think we're mature adults. God, I hope I am. Let's just put this behind us."

"That's very generous of you." He knew his speech was formal, but that was the only place he felt comfortable at the moment. Trying to ease the awkwardness, he added, "Wanna go see if there's plasma on the ice yet?"

She chuckled at his euphemism for a down-and-dirty hockey fight. "Sure."

She returned to the luxury box window and leaned over the open sill. Ross stared at the view.

Get it behind them, she'd said. How could he when she had such a great tush?

Chapter Two

"Oh, my God. What happened?"

Elaine stared down at the blood oozing from her forefinger. She sighed. "I was cutting carrots, Mom."

Her mother sighed, also. In exasperation. "I told you I would do that."

"But I wanted to help," Elaine explained, as her mother examined the cut. She wrinkled her nose. "Mom, I'm almost thirty years old, and I'm tired of being helpless in the kitchen."

"You will always be helpless in the kitchen. You take after your father," Mary Baransky replied, while getting a Band-Aid from the box on the kitchen sink shelf. "He got two left thumbs the moment he crossed the threshold."

Probably that was part of it, Elaine thought. She had no talent in this room. The other part was her mother, who treated the house as her domain over which she held dictatorship rights. Neither Elaine nor her father ever did anything to her satisfaction, so Mary did it all herself. The arrangement made for a happy family. At least she and her dad were happy to get out of work.

But this Sunday dinner, Elaine had felt...different. Domesticated somehow. She hadn't been able to rid herself of the notion that Ross Steadwell was more adequate in running a household than she.

She must be losing her mind.

"You never help, honey. You know better. What prompted this?"

"Idiocy. Ouch! You wrapped the strip too tight, Mom."

Her mother snorted. "You always say that."

"Yeah, when my finger falls off for lack of blood supply, then how will you feel?"

"As if the strip was too tight. I'll save the guilt trip for when that happens. And you haven't answered my question. What prompted this?"

Elaine shrugged as she adjusted the bandage to a wrap that wouldn't leave her nine-fingered for life. "I just wanted to be helpful. You're not getting any younger, Mom."

Her mother eyed her. "You are really beginning to irritate me."

Elaine grinned. "Only now?"

"Get out." Her mother shooed her from the kitchen.

Elaine sat down on the family sofa and mindlessly stared at the television set. Her father, glued to his football game, never said a word. In the companionable silence, Elaine admitted she knew what had prompted her venture into no-sane-woman's land. An odd need for domesticity. She could put together a forty-million-dollar deal with great finesse, but she could not put a roast beef and vegetable dinner on the table without a tragedy.

Domesticity had never stirred before until Ross and his two children walked into her office. Until Ross kissed her. Elaine shivered, all hot and cold at the remembered feel of his lips on hers. Never had she

crossed the barrier before between business and personal relationships. Never had she thought it would
happen as quickly as that. They had straightened it out
in the aftermath, but she now had to face him at a lunch
tomorrow. Elaine drew in a mind-clearing breath. She
had made two mistakes in her life with men, mistakes
that had made her stronger and wiser. She could handle
any future meetings with Ross. She *would*.

But the next day, when Ross rose from his seat at
the White Dog Café, Elaine knew she was in trouble.
He just looked so damn good with his dark hair brushing his pristine white collar and his easy smile. He put
out his hand for her to shake as she reached their table.
His fingers closed around hers, so warm and inviting
yet strong and reassuring that Elaine's knees turned to
jelly. *Help me,* she thought, knowing she had already
lost control of her reasoning powers.

"Hi," he said, in that smooth, gritty voice that went
right through her heart.

"No kids today?" she asked, teasing, although she
wished they were here. Anything to distract her.

"I've got baby-sitters galore," he replied, releasing
her hand. "I dropped Ariel off at my mother's store
and someone's picking Jimmy up from school." He
chuckled. "No distractions today."

That's what you think. Elaine sat down at the table.
"What's for lunch? I'm starved."

Ross motioned to a waiter as he resumed his seat.
"Whatever you want."

"No salad," Elaine decided. "I want real food today."

"My mother would like you," Ross said, grinning.
"She says women who eat like rabbits are rabbits."

"I think I like your mom. You said she owns a store?"

"It was the family hardware store until my dad died a few years back. She made it a combination hardware store and coffee bar. It's a place to hang out and buy ten-penny nails at the same time."

"What a nifty idea," Elaine said, fascinated that two diverse things would go together. "Is it profitable?"

"Absolutely. She holds workshops for women on household repairs."

"I bet that's where your Daddy Club meets, isn't it?"

"Right. I suppose that wasn't hard to guess. Actually the club was my mother's idea."

"Your mom sounds creative and innovative. Tell her send me a résumé."

"Over my dead body. RP Computers would get her first. But don't tell her that."

Free and easy, Elaine thought, relieved the conversation was flowing, although she still felt an undercurrent of sexual tension running along her veins, caused just by being in his presence. She hoped he couldn't tell. She hoped he suffered the same. She hoped she wasn't this wishy-washy when it came time to close any deal with RP Computers.

"Oh, Lord," she muttered, knowing she was losing it.

Ross frowned. "Is there a problem?"

"No, no, just thinking about the hockey game the other night."

As soon as the words left her mouth, Elaine knew she'd been a dummy of major proportions to even bring the event up. Heat flooded her cheeks until she felt she was burning up.

"I meant the stupid call by the referee," she corrected.

She realized she was breathing rapidly, and her lungs were expanding like a bellows. She never could lie well.

"Ah, here's drinks!" she said cheerfully as the waiter arrived with a laden tray.

Too bad it was only sparkling mineral water. She needed a real drink, big-time.

"To hockey games," Ross said wryly, lifting his glass.

Elaine chuckled and clinked her glass with his. "To hockey games."

"I'm interested in what your information base will require," he said, getting down to business.

"I've brought more preliminary specs, to see if your company can match up with this part," she commented, getting out papers from her briefcase.

"We'll match up anything," Ross promised.

They leaned over the papers she put between them on the table. Elaine found herself getting a whiff of his cologne. It reminded her of the sea on a crisp day, tangy and biting. She wondered if he would taste tangy. She couldn't help noticing his fingers were long and slim. His palms had faint calluses and she wondered how a salesman got them. Usually men in management had baby hands, soft and pudgy.

She tried to ignore his hands as they talked further about the exact needs of Data, Ink, but every movement seemed to draw her attention even more.

"How did you get those calluses?" she asked abruptly.

Ross blinked. "What? Where?"

"On your hands." She paused. "I'm sorry. I'm being an idiot."

"Okay." He grinned at her.

She sighed. "Since I'm halfway there…how *did* you get those calluses on your hands? Most salesmen don't have them. I notice things. Bear with me."

"I come from hardware stock. I *have* to have calluses."

It clicked in her head about his mother owning a hardware store. "Right. Dummy me. Sorry. I'm not sure a four-gig hard drive will do the job for the desktops—"

"How did you get the bandage on your finger?"

She blinked this time. "What? Oh. I cut myself helping my mother with Sunday dinner."

He frowned and took her hand. "It must be deep."

Something was deep all right, and it wasn't the cut on her hand. Ross's touch sent a spiral of sensations through her. She tried to breathe, but air refused to enter her lungs. She tried to move but her body was too intent on the heat rushing through her system. It pooled deep inside her until she only wanted to shift restlessly and stir the feelings even more.

She realized he was speaking. "What?"

At least her voice worked. Barely.

"Did you go to the hospital for it?" he asked.

"No." She frowned and pulled her hand away. The act had "graceless" written all over it, but she couldn't help herself. God knows what she would do if he continued to touch her like this. Probably fling herself at him and take him down for the most ferocious kiss of both their lives. "No. It's not bad. Just your average cut-your-finger-instead-of-the-carrot. I don't know why

I keep trying in the kitchen. My mother says I'm hopeless."

"Nobody's hopeless." He grinned at her. "That's my mother's theory. Just to back it up she holds those courses I told you about. Even I get roped in. I'm teaching one on planing doors tomorrow night."

"Really?" Elaine made a mental note of it. "You get along well with your mother, don't you?"

"Yeah." He flushed slightly. "She's great, but I would never tell her that because she'd be such a pain in the neck about it. But I would have been lost without her when my wife died. My mother and some of her customers kept things going for me and the kids. She still does, except when she eats a batch of old cannoli. She and her friends, my baby-sitting backups, all ate some of the stuff when they went gambling in Atlantic City. They all got so sick they thought they were dying. But that's how my kids wound up in your office that day—all my baby-sitters gave themselves a bad dose of food poisoning." He grinned widely. "A fact that will pay off handsomely for you and Data, Ink. I'm going to work overtime to give you the best deal and the best service just because you didn't throw me out of your office that day."

Elaine smiled archly. "I'll hold you to that...provided we *can* deal. RP has a long way to go." Her smile turned sweet. "Anyway, your mother sounds like an interesting woman."

"Would you like to meet her? I have to pick my kids up after our lunch today, and her store isn't far. About a half hour from here."

The implications of meeting a man's mother flitted through Elaine's brain, but she dismissed them. She was only interested in meeting a woman who was so

clearly self-made and creative, on the cutting edge.
She'd always felt women like that cleared the way for
women like her, although Ross's mother balanced business and family, something Elaine wouldn't have to
face. Not with her domestic track record.

"I'd love to," she said, forgetting all about business.

A short time later she found herself face-to-face with
a small-boned woman whose short salt-and-pepper hair
massed around her face. Her blue eyes, so like Ross's,
twinkled merrily at her. Her handshake was as strong
as a man's. Elaine had been expecting someone taller
and less amused looking, but the firm grip revealed the
woman's soul. Ruth Naomi Steadwell had clearly
weathered many things in her life and was doing just
fine.

"Hi," Ruth Naomi said, her voice husky and deep,
a more feminine version of Ross's. "I've heard a lot
about you, mainly that I ought to be grateful you didn't
toss Ross and my grandbabies out on their cabooses."

Elaine chuckled, although she found it disconcerting
that Ross had spoken about her to his mother. "Ross,
yes, the kids, no. Ross has spoken about you and the
store. I wanted to see it. I have great admiration for a
woman business owner."

"In this day and age of conglomeration and strip
malls, one needs to have an admiration of *any* business
owner." Ruth Naomi grinned, taking any sting out of
her formal words. "Hell's bells, honey, you interested
in starting your own business? Here's some free advice:
Don't do it."

Elaine laughed. "Actually I'm interested in taking
over Data, Ink, when my boss retires. I figure in about
ten years."

"And Ross has an in now. Smart thinking, son!"

Ruth Naomi called over to the coffee bar where Ross was sitting with his children.

"What, Mom?" he asked, frowning in puzzlement.

Elaine and Ruth laughed. Ruth began to show her around the store, clearly very proud of it. Well she should be, Elaine admitted, admiring the neat well-stocked shelves and bins, the wide aisles that held everything from power saws to copper roofing nails. The coffee bar in the back of the store, with its brightly lit bakery cases and art deco furnishings, bustled with business. People sat at tables or at the counter, reading the day's newspapers and magazines, while they sipped coffee and noshed on beautifully presented pastries.

"I hear the cannoli's to die for," Elaine said with a straight face.

"That little sneak told you that?" Ruth Naomi groused, casting an eye to her son who must have towered over her before he turned twelve. "Margie, Ula Mae, a couple of other friends and I thought the cannoli looked great in a little bakery's window. It was three in the morning. Why we thought we could see straight, and why we ate cannoli that had been in a window display, unrefrigerated for hours even though it was November, I don't know."

Elaine could envision a carload of Ruth Naomi look-alikes laughing and eating tepid cannoli on their way home from a night of gambling. It was a recipe for gastronomic disaster. Poor Ross. He must have been beside himself when all his baby-sitters turned up violently ill, she thought in amusement. She'd earned more brownie points than she'd known when she had accepted him and his children into her office.

"Hi, lady!" Ariel raced up to her and threw her arms around Elaine's knees. The little girl, filled with enthusiasm, nearly knocked her over. She did knock Elaine's emotional breath from her at the greeting.

"Hi, Ariel," Elaine said, awkwardly patting Ariel on her back. The child felt delicate, like a fledgling bird or a kitten, so young and helpless.

"Did you bring me something?" Ariel asked Elaine, her tone expectant as she let go of Elaine's legs.

"Ah...not this time," Elaine said. The little girl's face fell, and Elaine added, "Next time I will, okay? I don't have children of my own so I didn't know."

"Okay." Ariel smiled happily.

"You are a greedy child," Ruth Naomi admonished. "If I were Elaine, I wouldn't bring you a thing except myself."

"Okay," Ariel said. She grinned at Elaine. "Next time you bring you, okay?"

"Okay." Elaine grinned at the child, wondering if she'd have to get a life-size dummy of herself to satisfy Ariel's demand. She was in big trouble.

Ross and Jimmy came over to them. Ross looked relaxed and calm, a little different from the socially adept salesman she knew. She realized she was seeing a side of him that she'd only glimpsed in his interspersed talk of family. Ruth Naomi's rough affection had bred a man who was content with himself. It was obvious that his children meant everything to him, and he did what he did in business to keep this life going.

Elaine had never had that for herself. The notion that she was missing something important bothered her.

Ariel announced her gift for Elaine's next visit. Jimmy said nothing, just looked at her.

Elaine swallowed. "I'll bring you a little race car. How's that?"

Jimmy grinned.

"No you will not," Ross said sternly, then lectured both his children on the propriety of gifts. Jimmy and Ariel looked unrepentant, then looked at Elaine as if to say, "Hey, our commitment stands, lady."

Elaine sighed. Ruth Naomi snorted with wry amusement. Elaine noticed a sign announcing an upcoming class, the one Ross had mentioned at lunch. She made a note of the time and date.

Yes, it was going to be interesting getting to know this other side of Ross.

"OKAY, LADIES, you run this over the surface. Lightly."

Ross ignored the "oooo" of sensuality from his audience. The Hardware for Women Koffee Klatch consisted of former class clowns trying to revive their art form. Most of the forty or so women in the room were earnest about learning how to do home improvements, but his mother's friends always added "spice" when he ran a workshop. He never knew whether to shoot them or thank them. Right now he was in a shooting mood.

To dispel it, he moved the plane down the edge of the door. "Not too hard. Just one long, smooth stroke."

"Be still my heart!" Ula Mae called out.

"Look out, world, I have a pulse again," another added.

"I believe his father said that to me a time or two," Ruth N. commented thoughtfully.

Ross lost his poise, cutting a large chip out of the door in the process. It went flying across the room…right into Elaine's hands.

She stood at the edge of the class area, dressed in jeans and a gray fleece shirt. Her hair was loose and curling around her shoulders. Eyebrows shooting up, she said, "Does this mean I've caught the bouquet?"

Everyone laughed.

"I know I'm late for class, but you don't have to throw things at me, Ross," Elaine said, walking over to an empty seat in the back row.

She tossed the wood chip back at him. He caught it with one hand. Everyone applauded.

"You came to take the class?" he asked, not caring that he had listeners.

She shrugged. "I thought I might. Is that okay?"

"Of course it is," Ruth Naomi broke in. She turned to her son. "I told you she signed up the other day when she was here."

No, you didn't, Ross thought, although he kept his mouth shut. If he responded, his mother would have some smart remark—the woman thrived on them—that would rile up the class. Retreat was the better part of smart remarks.

"Welcome to the class," he said, smiling at Elaine. "I just started planing the door here..." He rapped on the thick panel sitting on two saw horses.

"It's one long, smooth stroke for man," Marge volunteered from the coffee bar.

"One great moment for womankind," Ruth N. added, grinning.

"Don't mind them," Ross said to Elaine. "They have dirty minds and lack of—"

"Watch it, boy," his mother warned.

"As I was saying...one long, smooth stroke." Ross grinned, then planed the door properly. "Be sure to take it off the end, not the middle, otherwise you'll have a funky-looking door. If you have a hollow door, and if your home was built in the sixties or after, then you probably do. Frankly, you're in trouble if you have to plane off more than a few eighths of an inch.''

Elaine raised her hand. ''I have hollow doors. At least they sound hollow to me. What do I have to do then?''

''Cut a hole in the wall,'' Ross quipped.

''Really?''

Everyone started laughing again. Elaine looked puzzled, then grinned ruefully. ''Okay, now you all know. I'm carpentry-deficient.''

''Just call one, honey, and carpenters come out to the house,'' Ula Mae told her. ''You can watch 'em plane all day long.''

''Then why are you here?'' Elaine asked.

''It's more fun when you plane together. You've got a lot to learn.''

''I feel like I walked into a dirty movie,'' Elaine said, shaking her head.

''Stick around, it gets dirtier,'' Ross replied. ''Now that you've seen planing, who would like to try it? You never know when a carpenter won't show.''

''I think Elaine should come up,'' Ruth said.

''Mom,'' Ross muttered, seeing the gleam of matchmaking in his mother's eye.

''I couldn't,'' Elaine said, but was urged by her fellow class members to be the first.

Ross watched as Elaine walked toward him, her hips unconsciously swaying in a way that warmed his blood. Her jeans only emphasized her slender thighs and the junction of her legs. Even her shirt contributed by falling to just above that sweet triangle. Ross's legs refused to move. He hoped nothing gave away his own reaction to her. How would he work with this woman over the coming weeks on an all-important proposal when he turned rock hard just looking at her?

He was a widower, barely past the mourning stage. How could he have these thoughts, especially so strongly? He felt like a traitor and yet not a traitor.

"What do I do?" Elaine asked, breaking into his reverie.

Ross cleared his throat—and hated the giveaway gesture. He gripped the plane and held it up for all to see. "Take the plane like this...hand on the knobs, here and here. You set it against the area you wish to reduce, then push."

"One long, smooth stroke!"

"Thank you, Mom." He handed over the plane to Elaine.

She took it awkwardly. "Like this?"

"Not really."

He put his hand over hers. Her flesh was warm, soft, her fingers small and slim. They gripped the knob with surprising strength, however. He wondered if she would grip him the same way.

Ross growled in the back of his throat, disgusted with himself.

"I beg your pardon?" Elaine asked.

"I have a tickle," he muttered, prying her fingers loose from their wrong position and putting them right. They slid the plane along the door edge.

"We're sliding now, Marge," Ula Mae said.

Elaine blushed lightly. Ross wondered if her thoughts matched his: just plain lustful. He hoped so. He hated to think he was in this alone.

On her own, Elaine gave a halfhearted push. She stopped. "It won't go."

"Push harder," Ross urged.

Ruth Naomi said. "Just like his father."

"Mom!"

"What?" his mother asked, all innocence. "I'm talking doors, son. What are you talking?"

Elaine laughed with the rest of the room, although her blush seemed darker. Ross admitted that despite having one's mother announce her former marital life to the world, he liked Elaine's good-natured acceptance of the older ladies' playfulness.

Elaine tried again. She moved farther along, but the plane suddenly tumbled to the floor. Everyone gasped, and Ross jumped out of the way of the plane that shouldn't be flying.

"See?" Elaine said, pointing to the tool. "I'm hopeless."

"No, you're not." Ross bent and picked up the plane. "I'll help you get started again."

This time he came around behind Elaine. Stretching his arms over her, he took her hands one at a time and placed them properly on the plane. He then bent with her and pushed on the tool.

"There," Ross said in Elaine's ear. "How was that?"

"Perfect," she murmured in return.

It felt perfect, he thought, breathing in the scent of sandalwood and woman.

The class suddenly applauded. Ross straightened, astonished by the reaction—and terrified he'd given himself away.

"Nice demonstration, son," Ruth said, clapping her hands together.

Ross eyed the arch of his mother's brow. He had the distinct feeling she saw through him like a piece of cellophane wrap. Nothing was more disconcerting than to be caught in a compromising thought by one's own mother.

"Hell," he muttered.

"Thank you, thank you, everyone. And for my next selection…"

Whoa! Who's the babe, Ross?"

The male voice penetrated the hardware store, its tones booming off the walls. Micah Steadwell looked over the group, straight at Elaine. Ross's older brother held his niece on his one shoulder, Tiny Tim style. Ariel wrapped her little hand around her uncle's forehead as she grinned at her father through her thumb. Jimmy had a smear of what looked like dark syrup on his cheek and a contented smile on his lips. Ross had a feeling the walk on which Micah had taken the kids had included a stop at the ice cream parlor half a block away.

"I had ice ceam, Daddy," Ariel announced, after popping her thumb out of her mouth. "Uncle Micah says you gotta eat ice ceam every day."

"So how come we don't?" Jimmy demanded.

"Because Uncle Micah has a crazy view of the world," Ross said. "I've told you that before."

The audience laughed, clearly enjoying this sideshow.

"Ah, the ant speaks once again about the grasshopper's life-style," Micah mused, setting his niece down. "I lead a musician's life. What do you expect? And you haven't answered my question. Who's this lovely lady?"

"This is Elaine Baransky, who is also a prospective client of RP Computers as well as a class member, so be on your best behavior." Ross stared pointedly at Mic.

"God, you make me sound like a jerk where women are concerned," his brother complained jovially. "I got over that when I was sixteen."

"What about Carla?" their mother asked.

"Okay, so I reformed after last year." Micah smiled broadly at Elaine as he shook her hand.

"Yeah, Dad, let me try!" Jimmy suddenly said, smiling up at his father as he ran to Elaine for the plane.

"No," Ross began.

"Here," Elaine said right on his heels, taking the plane from Ross and holding it out for Jimmy.

The boy grabbed for the tool, swiping it out of Elaine's hands before he could be stopped. The sudden heaviness of the plane spun Jimmy in a half circle.

Ross took up the plane from the boy before anyone got hurt. "Tools are not toys, guys. And they are not to play with. Mom, take this thing while we go on to sanding."

After the workshop, everyone retired to the coffee bar for the Koffee Klatch part of the lecture.

Elaine gave Ariel a little stuffed version of Fluff-balls, the latest doll craze. She gave Jimmy a set of racing cars. Ross wasn't sure he approved of gifts because they spoiled the kids, but let it go. When he would have asked Elaine to have coffee with him, his brother got in the request first.

Instead of butting in and joining them—his brother's lack of invitation to him apparent—Ross parked at the counter with his kids. He watched Micah monopolize Elaine. Ross glowered darkly when Elaine smiled at his brother. His brother was Peter Pan, the forever boy, who only wanted to play guitar in a rock and roll band.

Ross wanted nothing more than to punch the forever boy right in the kisser.

And Micah better not even *think* of doing that.

"Daddy, I don't want this." Ariel shoved a chocolate chip cookie practically up his nose.

"Honey, I eat these things with my mouth, not with my nose."

"I don't want mine, either," Jimmy said, tossing his onto the counter.

"Then why did you take it?" Ross asked.

Jimmy shrugged.

"As your grandmother would say, 'Eyes bigger than the stomach.'"

Jimmy crossed his eyes in an unconscious attempt to confirm the old saying.

"Never mind, son." Ross patted him on the back. An idea popped in his head as he noticed Elaine tilting her coffee cup up to drain it. "Why don't you go over and give the cookies to Uncle Micah. He's always hungry."

The kids brightened. They retrieved their cookies and headed over to their uncle, ready to palm the unwanted treats off onto the garbage pit that talked.

"Don't forget to shove it up his nose," Ross advised. "Your uncle doesn't smell so good in his old age."

Sibling rivalry never died, Ross thought without shame. The weapons just changed over the years.

Ross ambled over as his kids affectionately attacked their uncle with their cookies. As he surmised, Micah became preoccupied with entertaining the two while eating their offered treats.

He put his hand on Elaine's elbow and urged her up. "Micah won't be into adulthood again for about a half hour. Come on and I'll show you how to hang the door you just planed.''

Elaine grinned, slipping to her feet. ''Wow. Two lessons in one tonight. I bet you do that to all your students.''

''You'd bet wrong.''

When they cleared the coffee bar area and were well within the rows of hardware shelves, Elaine said, ''I'm sorry I gave Jimmy that metal car. I didn't realize he could get hurt with it.''

''No harm done,'' Ross said. ''You really are a novice with children.''

Elaine screwed up her face in a rueful expression. ''I'm a novice with everything domestic.''

The aisle was empty, just birdhouses and bags of seed as witnesses. Ross could see the lift of Elaine's chin, the slight parting of her mouth when she drew in a deep breath. He could almost feel the pressure change between them. The curves of her breasts enticed him for his touch. He knew he shouldn't. He shouldn't even be this close to her, thinking these thoughts. Sex and business didn't go hand in hand. Besides, he was a man with a lot of baggage and he knew it.

But her lips parted even more and the tip of her tongue moistened them in a move as natural as it was breathtaking. The baggage found shelves to settle into as did his common sense. Ross leaned forward and pressed his lips to hers, tasting their sweetness. Her mouth dipped and moved with his for an endless moment before their tongues met in a gentle duel. Ross put his hands on Elaine's arms, his thumbs just brushing against her breasts. He moved them deliberately along the side swell, feeling their softness under her clothing. Elaine shivered at the touch, her mouth deepening the kiss. Her fingers dug into his arm muscles, the nails reminding him of a kitten's claws, gentle and yet demanding.

His common sense fell off the shelf where it had hidden itself, not with a bang but with a whimper. Ross realized the moan had come from him. He eased his mouth away, then stepped back. "I don't know what to say."

Elaine's mouth looked swollen, pouty. He nearly kissed her again, the urge so strong and overwhelming.

"I… Me, neither, so let's not worry about it." She smiled a little. "This is a different situation, more on a personal side."

"I suppose something was bound to erupt," Ross said, thinking it would be him through his jeans. Man, but he had innuendo bad. "To get us back to business, we do need another spec meeting."

"I know." She sounded as reluctant as he felt. "Thursday? My office?"

"Sure. I'll call Tina to set up a time."

"Fine."

He walked her the rest of the way to the door in silence. Much as he wanted to walk her to her car, just to be a gentleman, he knew he wouldn't stay that way for long if they were alone in the dark. When he opened the door and she slipped through it, he said, "I'll see you Thursday."

"Right."

She was gone in a moment, down the street. He saw a light come on in a car parked partway down the block. It started up and drove past. Elaine didn't wave.

Ross sighed.

"Hey, I'm sorry." Micah looked contrite and a little worried as he came up the aisle. His brother hadn't seen the kiss, otherwise the comment would have been entirely different.

"Mom told me just now about the big project you're working on with Elaine. She says it's huge," Mic added. "I promise it'll be hands off with Elaine from now on."

Ross wondered if he could say the same.

Chapter Three

Elaine frowned as she thought of the words Ross had used. She knew he was absolutely right, and she had absolutely no doubt she'd never achieve it with this man.

Could she have thrown herself at him any faster than she had after the workshop? She hoped not. She hoped she never did it again.

She was still hoping when Tina announced Ross for their second spec meeting. He came into the room and seemed to send a sexual energy straight toward her. The notion was silly, but as Elaine stared into his intense gaze she felt heat surge along every part of her body.

She shook her head to clear the sensations and rose to her feet. Extending her right hand to shake his, she thought better of it and gestured toward a visitor's chair. It would be a dangerous thing to touch, even for politeness, a man one was attracted to. "Please. Sit down."

Ross sat, but that left his upper body very visible to her. She wondered what it would be like to touch his bare shoulders, to see if they were as wide as his suit jacket promised. She decided that she liked his tight jawline. It signaled strength, not stubbornness or, heaven forbid, repression. If a guy like Ross was repressed, women everywhere ought to hang up their partying shoes now. She bet he liked women in sexy underwear, the sexier and skimpier the better. She bet he kissed even better when he wasn't hurried or trying not to. She wondered if she would survive such a kiss....

"Elaine."

His voice, low and deep, shook her to her self-control foundations, an already shaky place where he was concerned. She could feel that voice in her ear, whispering her name in a throaty way that said she had stirred him to the breaking point.

"Has the company made a decision on whether they want hardware with an eight-gig drive or a ten?"

"Not yet." Her voice wasn't bad, although a little breathy, not a surprise when she could barely get air into her lungs. Did he have to be so sexy? Did he have to talk *hard*ware? "It depends on the software we want."

She knew what she wanted and it wasn't soft. Ross's expression looked puzzled and, worse, mundane. That popped her sensual bubble faster than any behavior logic could. Clearly, he was no more affected by her at the moment than he was affected by the man in the moon.

"Preliminarily, we need a bundle-and-server package that's going to handle the following..."

As she ran down the list of prospective specifications that he would have to meet to support the software solution Data, Ink, required, she felt like a true businesswoman, not a gangling, giggling schoolgirl, something she had never been. Okay, so she'd been married twice, yet both had logic behind the impulsiveness. She married right after college to create an independent adult life-style rather than for wild, passionate love. Her second marriage was not only a rebound reaction for feeling a failure at her first, but because of life-style compatibility. Those two events should have demolished any gangling and giggling she had left.

Ross was Mr. Business, which kept her on the straight and narrow throughout the meeting. As they finished, she sat back and said, "So we will need five hundred PCs delivered by April one. That would be to start. We expect to quadruple that within two years. The delivery date must be met, Ross, or RP forfeits the deal. No delays."

"I think we can deliver when and what you want," Ross said. "And you *will* get what you want from us. Dall Computers may look good on paper, but I'm hearing they don't deliver exactly what you order."

"It's happened to us," Elaine conceded, grinning wryly while thinking about their last order with the big computer company. Her technicians were still tearing their hair out over how incompatible the system was with theirs when it shouldn't have been. "We had to put in a lot of fixes. That's why I listened to Tina about your company. We'll need set-up service, and RP has a great reputation for that."

"I'll serve, believe me." He laughed, then sighed as he picked up a notepaper that fell from his briefcase while he was putting his spec sheets away. "Hell, here's that shopping list I needed yesterday. No wonder we had no milk this morning for breakfast."

Elaine almost made a comment about her mother shopping for her and why not get his to do his, then realized Ruth Naomi was hardly a caretaker mother.

"I'm barely keeping up with things," he added,

chuckling. "I forgot to do laundry, and Ariel had no underwear. She was thrilled, the little exhibitionist. When I dropped her off for my mother to watch while I'm here, she proceeded to show her grandmother and all the store customers how dumb her dad is."

Elaine laughed. She could imagine Ariel in all innocence proving her father's forgetfulness. "I think you do a marvelous job with the kids. I know I couldn't do it."

"Thanks, but you ought to see the train wreck that's gone through my house. Jimmy now wants to do T-ball in the spring, and I don't know how I'm going to get him back and forth to games. And Christmas is coming." He shuddered. "How do I shop for the kids? Where do I hide the presents? And how do I find the time to balance my checkbook? It's going to be a great Daddy Club workshop. If I get any members for the next meeting."

Elaine gazed at him, realizing his lament was a cry for a second parent in his life. She had spoken more truth than she'd thought when she'd told him she couldn't do it. Her solution to housework was to pay a service to come in and take care of her place. She could drive, but had no clue what a T-ball was. Why, she wondered, would they call it a ball when it was shaped in a T? She could easily balance a checkbook, but presents for children were beyond her. Knowing her penchant for domestic misstep, she'd probably buy a chemistry set that allowed a kid to blow up a house.

Ross shrugged. "I'm sorry you got caught with all that. I'm not a complainer by nature." He grinned. "At least I hope I'm not."

"You're fine," she assured him. The thought of what he must have gone through raised all her sympathies. She wanted to offer comfort in more than words, but knew that was something she could not do. "It's got to be difficult for you with your wife passing away. That's a terrible thing to happen to anyone, let alone the children. I truly admire you for all that you do."

He stared at her, his jaw set for a moment, then he said, "If we didn't have this desk separating us, and if we didn't have the strictly business agreement, I would give you a kiss that would send you spinning."

"I don't think you have to kiss me to do that," Elaine murmured, her voice betraying her emotions.

He grinned wolfishly, his expression so virile it melted her. Yet he said, "I think we're getting into the trouble zone. I think I don't care."

Elaine all but climbed over the desk, wanting nothing more than to claim that kiss and to kiss him in return so passionately that it would send *him* spinning. She wanted nothing more than to prove she was competent in *one* area.

When she didn't move, he stood. "Back to business. Thank you for the meeting, Elaine. I think I've got everything I need now to make a good presentation. It'll take us some time to get the proposal fine-tuned. When is it convenient for Data, Ink, to meet?"

"As soon as you're ready," she said, rising to her feet. Part of her was disappointed that he had gone back to business, but she realized it was her lack of response that had triggered it.

As they walked to the door, something urged her not to stay silent on the subject of "not caring." When he would have reached for the knob, she put her hand out and stopped him.

He turned to her, his gaze questioning.

"Ross, I..." She looked up at him. "To hell with it."

She put her hands up and cupped his face, bringing his mouth to hers. She kissed him with all the fervor that had been pent up inside her since she'd met this man. Even before.

If she took him by surprise, he didn't act like it. His tongue met hers, gently at first, the need suppressed. But she could feel it below the surface, seething inside him like it seethed inside her. She heard a dull thud and belatedly realized it was his briefcase dropping to the floor. The passion exploded between them.

Ross snaked an arm around her waist and pulled her to him. Elaine pressed against him, trying to absorb him into her flesh. His chest was a hard wall, his waist taut and his hips narrow. Her pelvis would cradle him easily in its embrace. His thighs brushed hers intimately, sending hot shock waves through her body. His mouth was like sweet fire, a rich heat that shook her to her toes. She ran her hands through his hair, gripping the strands tightly as a helpless moan erupted from deep within her. His palms slowly ran up and down her spine as if memorizing each shifting movement during the kiss. His fingers touched her breast, exploring the side swell before caressing her already tight nipple. Her clothes couldn't mask the sensations he created, and she could only imagine how much stronger they would be if she were naked. She'd never survive it.

Rising on tiptoe, she dug her fingers in his shoulders, wanting to feel the hard muscles resist the pressure. His skin, even with a shirt and suit jacket, was already hot. She could feel the warmth through the layers. She wanted to feel all of him, warm flesh over hard muscles, explore every inch to see if he were as intriguing a male as she knew he must be.

He eased his mouth away but only to plant a string of satisfying kisses from ear to throat, hitting every sensitive nerve along the way. He returned to her mouth, caressing her lips with his, lightly at first, then with a second full kiss that took all the strength from her legs. She sagged into him, every bone in her body dissolving until she had no will, nothing but the kiss to end all kisses.

When they finally let go of each other, minutes and minutes later, Elaine leaned back against the door, still needing support for her body. Ross's hair was a mess, his jacket actually had crease marks from where her fingers had knotted the material and, best of all, his mouth looked thoroughly kissed. Elaine grinned with pleasure.

"I'm not apologizing this time," he said, grinning back.

"Neither am I."

"Good."

"Before you go, you better fix your hair and wipe your mouth." She knew she had a smirk on her face, and she wasn't about to get rid of it, proud that she had left her mark on him.

He glanced up as if he could see what his hair looked like, then gave up and brushed his hair into place with his fingers. Elaine took his handkerchief from him, after he had taken it out of his pocket, and wiped her lipstick off his mouth. She sighed a little unhappily when he was presentable again.

"I think you looked cuter the other way," she said.

He chuckled, then wiped her mussed lipstick from

her lips with his handkerchief. "Keep talking like that and I'll kiss you again."

"I know." When he arched his brow, she added, "I'll be good."

"That's what I'm afraid of," he muttered, putting the now-stained square of material away.

He didn't say when he would see her again, other than the meeting, or if he even would see her socially. She didn't ask. Somewhere she knew she was crossing a line that shouldn't be crossed, but she wasn't willing to acknowledge it.

She still wasn't willing to acknowledge it on Saturday, when she was shopping at the local mall with her mother and they ran into Ross and his children.

Ariel ran to her and wrapped her arms around her legs. Elaine patted the child's back, not quite knowing what to do other than that. Her mother looked on with arched eyebrows. Ross's greeting was more sedate. Jimmy didn't look at her.

"Daddy, it's that lady," Ariel said, letting go of Elaine.

"Yes, I know." Ross smiled at her, then prompted Jimmy with a push on the back.

"Hi," Jimmy said finally, looking up from the racing car that preoccupied him. "Dad bought me another one that goes with the one you got me."

Elaine smiled. "That's good."

"Yeah." Jimmy returned to his car perusal.

Mary Baransky gazed at Ross, clearly assessing him as a man. Elaine suppressed a grin. She supposed her mother could appreciate a virile-looking man as much as any woman could. Only it was weird to see it happening.

"Mom, this is Ross Steadwell. Ross, my mother, Mary."

"It's a pleasure to meet you, Mrs. Baransky." He shook hands with her mother, his gesture courtly. Even more courtly, he said, "You have a lovely daughter, and I'm not saying that because I want her company's business."

Elaine's face heated. Her mother looked bemused. Ross's voice, turned on its victim, had its usual impact. Mary glanced from Ross to Elaine, and suddenly her expression was far from bemused.

"Thank you," she said. "It's nice to meet my daughter's customers."

"He's not a customer, Mom," Elaine corrected, feeling a little like a streetwalker. *Customers.* What a notion. "He's a seller."

"If I'm lucky." Ross grinned at her and put his hand out. Elaine steeled herself and took it. His fingers squeezed hers meaningfully before he let go.

She wanted to reach out and hold it again, just to feel his strength and warmth. God, she thought, and right in front of her mother, too.

"We're shopping for underwear," Ariel announced, then popped her thumb in her mouth.

"Thank you," Ross said to his daughter. "And thanks for retreating now, that you've embarrassed me and your brother thoroughly."

Ariel frowned, but clearly wasn't curious enough to ask what he meant.

"Dad turned our underwear a sissy pink," Jimmy told them. Amenities may not have been the boy's specialty, but he spoke when he thought it relevant. Clearly his father's boo-boo with the laundry was relevant.

"I'd thank you, too, but it would go over your head," Ross told his son.

Jimmy frowned. "What?"

"Never mind. Shopping today?" he asked in general. "Anyone else turn their underwear pink in the wash lately? Which wouldn't have happened if I hadn't missed that red soccer shirt of yours from the last load, my son."

"You gotta buy me a new soccer shirt, Dad."

"Lovely child," Ross muttered. He shook himself and grinned.

Elaine decided to help him out. "I've turned a few laundries pink, haven't I, Mom?"

"Oh, yes. She never has grasped reading the directions on a detergent bottle."

"Hey, dry cleaners love me," Elaine protested.

Her mother laughed. "I know."

"We're shopping for new curtains for me," Elaine said, giving him an explanation for their presence. "My mom likes to help."

"Your mother knows you have no clue," Mary said. "Left to yourself, you would buy heavy, lined drapes for a kitchen window."

"Well, I might want some privacy," Elaine defended.

Ross laughed and said to her mother, "Wanna trade?"

"I'll think about it."

The kids got antsy, Ariel pulling on her father's hand, to get him moving. They said goodbye and parted company, Ross and his family heading in the opposite direction from the "best shop for curtains in New Jersey," according to her mother.

Mary turned to Elaine. "He was…interesting."

"Oh, look, there's the shop!" Elaine said brightly.

The distraction, however, didn't last beyond the walk to the place.

"There's something going on with you and that man, isn't there?" her mother asked, as soon as they were in a quiet area of the store.

"No. What do you think of this, Mom?" Elaine held up a bright blue curtain with lots of puppies and kittens on it.

"That's for a baby boy's room."

Elaine dropped the curtain. "Oh."

"He seems nice enough," Mary said. "And he's got a terrific voice. Smooth and rough at the same time. A woman could hear that day and *night*."

Elaine covered her face with her hands, trying to keep the flood of humiliating heat from flowing right out of her face. "God, Mom."

Mary laughed. "Thought that would get the truth out of you. So who is he?"

"Just what he said. He's a rep for a company that wants to do business with us."

"And is he married? Or divorced? He's something. He's got kids."

"He's a widower."

"Oh. That's too bad. When did he lose his wife?"

"Almost two years ago. What about these?" Elaine held up a bright-yellow curtain set with chicks on them.

"You're looking at nursery stuff again. My God, I hate to ask, but can't you tell the difference? Or are you telling *me* something?"

Elaine threw the curtains down. "No, I am not telling you anything."

"Okay." Her mother rooted through a bin of curtain sets. She pulled out one with a country motif. "This would look good in your kitchen. Or this. Or even this.''

Elaine looked at the ones pointed out to her.

"He's not for you, honey."

Elaine rounded on her mother, whose gaze was on the curtains. "What do you mean?"

"Elaine, you are a wonderful person and I am proud of you and all you've accomplished," her mother said, turning to her. "Never mistake that. But what that man needs is a wife and mother, not a career woman. That's what you are."

"Mom, you take things way too far," Elaine said, bristling at her mother's assessment. "You've just met him. How could you even know what he needs?"

"They were attached to his side, a boy and girl. A *little* boy and a *littler* girl. And I said what I say, because even you know you've never been good around little ones. Remember those occasions when you babysat for our neighbor? Every single time you had to call me to help you because the kids were acting up or something went wrong in the house. Elaine, you've been wise enough to know that sort of thing isn't your cup of tea. Much as I would love for you to give me grandchildren, I'm hoping you're wise enough to remember it now."

Elaine thrust out her chin, not willing to show that any of her mother's comments had hit the mark, let alone all of them. "Who said I'm going to marry the guy? Or anybody?"

"I haven't said such a thing."

"You sure sound like it, going on about wives and mothers. I'm telling you, Mom, you've got it all wrong. Ross is a business associate. Nothing more. Besides, he doesn't need a wife and mother. He's got this thing called The Daddy Club.''

She explained the club to her mother, even Ross's other workshops and his mother's hardware store concept.

Mary frowned, then shrugged. "Well, the home improvement lessons can't hurt you...as long as they have insurance out the kazoo. Knowing this, you're probably right about him *not* needing a chief cook and bottle washer."

"Even you have turned underwear pink in your time," Elaine reminded her.

"And so I have."

Her mother looked as unrepentant as Elaine felt.

ROSS LOOKED OUT across the workshop area, shocked to see men actually sitting in the seats.

"See?" his mother said archly, with a smug know-it-all expression on her face. "I told you to give the club time. You've got four here."

"Okay, so you're perfect and I'm not."

Ruth Naomi patted him on the back. "You got it. Finally."

Ross raspberried her, then went and greeted his true charter members of The Daddy Club. They might have missed the charter meeting, but they were charter members in his book. To his surprise every one of them was from Elaine's company. Bob was a tech, Clark a systems analyst, Tom a group manager and Arthur a maintenance supervisor.

"How did you hear about this?" Ross asked.

"Elaine Baransky." They voiced her name as one.

Ross further ferreted out that Elaine had not only mentioned the club, but had urged each one of them—

and others—in the company to attend the meeting as a cure-all for their single-parenting problems.

"It seems as if my kids come in, trash up my place, and by the time I've made them clean up they have to go home again," Clark said. "We're spending our little time together yelling at each other and cleaning their messes. It's not what I want to do with them, but I don't know how to get on a different tack."

"I feel like an idiot being here because I'm not a single dad, but my wife is going back to work part-time nights as a nurse. I'll be the baby-sitter, and I can't change a diaper without tossing my cookies," Bob, the youngest man, said. "I've got a six-month-old and I'm desperate."

"My fourteen-year-old is dating a kid who scares the daylights out of me, and I don't know what to do," Tom added. "I feel like I'm in an AA meeting. I have this urge to say, 'Hi, I'm Tom and I'm a lousy dad.'"

The men laughed. His mother's friends, sitting in the coffee bar, laughed louder. Ross gave them a cold stare. They looked as if they were about to throw themselves onto the floor, hysterical. Ross gave up, knowing incorrigibles when he saw them.

"I'm just separated from my wife. I have a fridge full of beer and nothing nutritious for my kids, according to my soon-to-be ex-wife, an event that can't happen fast enough for me," Arthur chimed in. "Hey, nice store. You guys sell fifteen-sixteenths screws?"

"Aisle four," Ruth Naomi piped up. Her cronies looked on with interest from the coffee bar. Clearly they were sitting back to see how The Daddy Club would fare.

Ross realized that Elaine had given him an opportunity far beyond prospective club members. These men could give a good impression of him within Data, Ink. If they felt he delivered here, in a simple workshop discussion, then they would speak favorably about him to those who made the decisions at the company. Maybe the group manager or the systems analyst had a voting influence at Elaine's company. Ross vowed to kiss Elaine more than senseless when he saw her again.

He talked with the men about their needs and about what he envisioned for The Daddy Club. They seemed to like the idea that they would be helping themselves find solutions to their problems. In fact, they gave him a whole list of workshops and talks they wanted as well as naming more men they knew would benefit.

"Okay, then," Ross said, feeling good as he wrapped up the first meeting. "We'll have a nutritionist so we know what's healthy and what's junk…"

"Corn chips don't count."

"You got it!" Ross pointed to Bob in agreement. "But we can afford to lose a few pounds by eating right, corn chips excepted."

"We should have another workshop about how to live forever and make our ex-wives nuts," Arthur added. Arthur clearly had a personal agenda. He was just starting down the road to single parenthood, so maybe that explained his attitude.

Ross grinned at the man. The old ladies would eat him alive. "We'll do a laundry lecture. I need that one." Jimmy still complained about his sissy underwear. "Teenage dating and how to survive it, and woodworking with the kids."

"It'll give me something to do with them," Clark said. Clearly taking the quick fix suggested, he added, "Tomorrow I'm hiring a cleaning service to come in Monday mornings. Let their mom teach 'em to clean."

"Don't forget getting us a divorce lawyer on men's rights, and how to watch the football game when the kids are there."

Ross wondered how long Arthur would last. "That's for our second meeting. Now for our third..."

"How about getting along with your wife," young Bob suggested.

"Can't be done," Tom quipped. Arthur high-fived him.

They all chuckled. To his mother's delight, the men spent money at the coffee bar, even buying pastries and muffins as carryout for their morning breakfasts. They also bought things at the hardware section. Arthur went hog-wild with screws.

"Not bad," Ruth Naomi said, when she counted the drawer after the men left and the store closed. "Those four guys brought in almost two hundred dollars. It takes all forty women at the Koffee Klatch workshops to do that well."

"Mom, will you take the kids home?" Ross asked. "I want to get Elaine and celebrate with a victory drink. She saved The Daddy Club."

"No problem, honey. I'm buying." His mother was in an expansive mood. "Get that divorce lawyer in here, and Arthur'll be a member for life."

"No kidding."

Ross raced for his car. He knew where Elaine lived. He'd made it a point to find out. He'd felt damn foolish at the time following that schoolboy urge.

Now it would pay off.

Chapter Four

Ross stood on her doorstep, a silly grin on his face.

At least, it looked silly as heck through the peephole, Elaine thought, swinging the door wide open.

"What are you doing here?" she asked, astonished that he knew where she lived. She wasn't as upset as she should be that a business associate had her address when she hadn't given it to him. Instead, she was pleased. This was Ross. Thank God she had on decent jeans and a Berber fleece top rather than the ratty T-shirts she often opted for at home. Thank God her hair and makeup were still decent. Thank God nobody and nothing had messed up her house.

The thanking of the Supreme Being could have gone on forever from her perspective, but she mostly thanked the Big Guy for just putting Ross at her threshold.

"I want to take you out for a drink," he announced, his silly grin growing even wider as she shut the door behind him.

He walked straight to her, caught her up in a big bear hug and spun her in a circle.

"Wow!" she exclaimed when he set her down on

Mother Earth again. "The drink would have been fine."

"Hardly." He kissed her, then kissed her again more thoroughly. Their bodies melded together even as their mouths did, the fire rising instantly. Finally Ross let her go. "That and a drink don't even come close to a thank-you for what you've done. Those guys you sent to The Daddy Club were great, and they spent money in the store. A lot of it. My mother's ecstatic with you."

"It's nice to know I'm on *some* mom's happy list," Elaine commented, not explaining her remark further. "How many came?"

"Four."

"That's all?" Elaine frowned, disappointed by the small number. "I can't believe only four of them showed up. I must have told at least ten in the office. We've got a slew of single dads."

"Four was a great starting point. Get your coat. Come on."

She laughed at his enthusiasm. If four made him this happy, wait until she got after more of the men at work. "Why not have a drink here? I've got some decent whisky a vendor gave me for Christmas back when I was in sales. That way I don't have to dress up."

"You sure?" he asked. "My mother's buying, and you look just fine. Perfect in fact."

She smiled in pleasure at his compliment. It was amazing how far a few kind words could go. Although, this man, with that voice, could read her his grocery list and she'd be flattered.

"Why go out?" she said, shrugging. "The bars will be crowded and noisy and we'll have to drive a ways to get to the nearest one. I've been saving this bottle, mostly for a special occasion and mostly because it seemed a sin to open it when I barely drink, anyway. But this is a very special occasion. It's Chivas.''

The expensive spirits label was enough for Ross. ''We can't let that spoil.''

''Buy the kids something your mother hates with the money she gave you,'' Elaine suggested.

''Good thinking.'' Ross shed his coat while Elaine went to get the whisky, ice and some glasses.

When they were seated and he had poured them a nice two-finger drink in their wide-cut glasses, he touched his to hers with a satisfying chink. ''Here's to The Daddy Club charter meeting, and to you, Elaine, who made it all possible.''

''Thank you,'' she said solemnly. ''So who came tonight?''

''Clark, Bob, Tom and Arthur.''

''Tom the salesman or Tom the manager?''

''Tom the manager.''

''Good. He's a nice guy who really is worried about his daughter and how to handle that whole thing.'' With a sly tone, she added, ''So how did you like Arthur?''

Ross laughed. ''He's a man with a focus, that's for sure.''

''If you were a woman and we were gossiping. I'd tell you he's a typical male chauvinist pig.''

''If you were a man and we were hitting a few on the golf course, I'd tell you he sets the standard to which all men should aspire.''

Elaine burst into laughter. ''I could see that. I'm so glad you're pleased. These guys will go back and say good things about the club, then more will come.''

''I hope so.'' He took another sip. ''Damn, but I feel

so good about that meeting. I think I'm a nurturer by nature. Hell, Arthur won't be happy I'm getting in touch with my feminine side so well. I don't think that guy even has one."

"Probably not, but you have *nothing* to worry about, believe me."

As Ross's body stilled and tension rose in the small space between them, Elaine would have liked to have claimed that she hadn't meant the words to be so personally provocative. But she knew she had. She knew the moment she opened that door she could be letting in more than a man who wanted to share a platonic moment with her. She welcomed it, though she knew she shouldn't.

Ross leaned across the space and kissed her, this time with less ebullience and more need. A lot of need. His tongue plunged into her mouth, completely capturing hers in a sensual duel that sent her common sense spiraling into oblivion.

His hands pulled her closer, squeezing the space between them into nothing. Elaine snaked her arms around his shoulders, her fingers digging past the cotton of his shirt to grip the hard muscles underneath.

His mouth was fire on hers, the heat burning her and matching her own desire at the same time. His hands cupped her breasts, his fingers massaging her nipples into tight pebbles. Elaine moaned at the pent-up pleasure deep inside her that sought relief. Ross pushed her shirt and bra aside, his palms rubbing against her bared flesh. He pushed her back against the sofa seat cushions and pressed kisses along the outer curves of her breasts, slowly circling around her nipples.

"I know I shouldn't be doing this," he whispered,

against her nipple, the breath of his voice on her flesh
sending shivers down her spine.

"Me, too," she gasped, squirming around while he
pulled the fleece top over her head. Her bra was shed
like water from a seal's coat. "Kiss me again."

He obliged, his mouth laving one nipple to a dia-
mond hard point. "I really did mean only to come and
take you out for a celebration drink."

"I know, I know. Here, lift your arms so I can get
your shirt off."

He raised his arms, eagerly helping her with the
awkward task.

His chest and torso were defined with muscles. A
swath of dark, silky hair arrowed down past his waist-
band.

"Oh, my," Elaine murmured, appreciating the view.

He chuckled. "Nobody ever said that before."

"Good. I like to be unique." She reached up and
ran her hands over his chest. The silky hairs tickled her
palms in the most delicious manner and sent sensations
through her nerve endings like warmed chocolate. She
knew she was far too aggressive but she couldn't help
herself. She had to touch.

He groaned, his voice so sexy it melted her inhibi-
tions even further. She leaned up and kissed him, her
tongue demanding a like response from him. Their
flesh met and melded, her breasts crushed by his chest.
He pulled her under him, his hands cupping her derriere. It would be nothing, she thought, to take this to
its inevitable end....

Common sense eventually surfaced through the
primitive urges. She eased away from the kiss even as
he did. Still entwined and still half naked, he leaned
his forehead against hers. His chest was like a bellows,

heaving air in and out of his lungs as if he'd run a mile in three minutes flat.

"I'm doing it again," he said. "I'm sorry—"

"*We're* doing it again," she interrupted. "It's very gallant of you to try to shoulder all the blame, but your shirt didn't come off all by itself. I do believe that was my department."

He relaxed against her and chuckled. Turning his head to face hers, he said, "I don't feel gallant. That's a helluva word, by the way."

"It's apt." She quirked her mouth and sighed. "So we've got a problem. We're attracted and we both have lots of reasons why we shouldn't be giving in to it."

"That's the nutshell." He was quiet for a minute, then said, "Look, our problem is that we're in negotiations." When she took a breath to speak up, he added, "Preliminary negotiations."

She grinned.

"I think the best thing we can do is to settle the business between us, one way or another, as soon as possible and then see if we've reduced the lots of other reasons for not getting involved."

She thought about his kids and her lack of domesticity. She hated the notion that her mother might be right, that she wasn't the woman for him. That she lacked the basic element he needed in a female.

In her core she knew she was far too competitive than she should be. That's partly what got her where she was at Data, Ink.

"I think that's a wonderful idea," she said. "What did you have in mind?"

"We've talked about waiting until I'm ready for a presentation. Hell, I'm ready now."

She giggled, feeling how ready he was. "Okay. How is next Monday? Provided I can set it up with Burt."

"Fine."

"I should warn you that Burt is unpredictable. Headstrong, impatient and extremely bright."

"Sounds like my mother." He shuddered. "That's the last person I should be talking about when I'm half-naked with a woman. I think the mood's killed now until after Monday at least."

"We can talk about my mother, but then the mood will be killed for about a year." She shivered at the thought of what her mother would say if she saw her like this with Ross.

"Then mothers are forbidden in our conversations. Unless we need the mood killers." He sat up and put his shirt on.

Not at all insulted by his change from a sexual being to a business one, Elaine scrambled for her top. When the fleece settled around her shoulders and down her body, she felt as if she'd successfully hidden her sexuality from the parental all-seeing eye. She was nearly thirty and she still couldn't avoid its imagined impact.

"Once a kid, always a kid," she said.

"Just what I was thinking." He grinned at her and pulled her over for a tender kiss. His lips were soft and yet virile at the same time. How, she wondered, her head already spinning with unfulfilled need, did he do that?

"Thank you again for the new membership, although I'm not sure about Arthur," Ross whispered in her ear.

If he told her she was the most beautiful woman he'd ever seen, she couldn't have felt a stronger shiver of anticipation. "You could read the *Wall Street Journal*'s

stock market pages and make it exciting. Where did
you get that voice?''

He smiled. ''Would you believe I had one so high-
pitched as a kid that my dad took me to the doctor to
make sure everything was in the right place.''

She laughed. ''No. You're kidding.''

He raised his right hand. ''I swear. And I better go.''

He got up and drained his glass. Elaine knew it
wasn't enough to worry that he was driving under the
influence. If he were, she would insist he stay. If he
did, well, who knew what might happen....

''You okay to drive?'' she asked hopefully, rising to
her feet. ''That was a fair-size glass you poured.''

''It was only two swallows,'' he replied, not getting
her point at all.

''Okay,'' she said, disappointed that he was absolutely right.

''You'll call me to confirm Monday for the presentation?''

She nodded.

''I hope the kids are angels this weekend.'' His expression was rueful. ''I've got a lot of work ahead of
me.''

''We could make it later,'' she offered.

''No. Hell, no. We've been naughty enough as it is,
with all this hanging over us. Let's get it done.''

He sounded so determined, she had to grin. It would
be interesting to see exactly what he put together for
Monday.

And then...then it would be interesting to see what
happened next.

''ALL SET?''

Ross adjusted the last chart in his notebook computer, to make sure it properly fed over to the proxima, a projector that took images directly from a computer and sent them onto the far wall. He nodded to Elaine. "All set."

"Good. They'll be here any minute. Good luck, Ross."

She had not only come through for a late-Monday-afternoon meeting with her boss, but she looked fabulous in a pants suit of a soft-gray color. The jacket fit her breasts and waist like a glove, and the trousers only emphasized her long slender legs. She wore matching shoes with squared toes and two-inch heels that harkened back to the seventies look. Her hair was wrapped intricately in chopsticks. Earlier, he had watched her pull the two things out, wind her hair around them, or maybe them around her hair, then shove them in diagonally through the tresses. Perfection.

He itched to pull the chopsticks out and see everything tumble free. Then unbutton that jacket and slip off those pants...

Ross smiled to himself. He was more than ready—with some guilty feelings, too. He tried to tell himself he shouldn't be, that he was allowed to have a life again with a woman, but he'd been a married man for too long and had been made single too abruptly to achieve an easy adjustment to a different status.

The other night had brought him closer to having that life. He hadn't been able to stop himself responding to Elaine, even with some holdover spousal guilt. She had met him at every turn, and it would have been so easy to go over the edge neither of them were sure about. Elaine *was* very different from Barbara, something that didn't make an echo of the past in the present. He wondered how well he would have done if he'd met Elaine before Barbara's passing. Better not to go there, he thought, glad he'd never been put to the test. Things happened when they happened, and he was grateful for that.

The door to the conference room opened and a long line of men filed in. Bringing up the rear was an older man around his mother's age. He was very fit and wore a gray suit with a bloodred tie. His hair was thin and he was balding, but the chomp of his jaw was square, barely jowly. It was easy to discern from his bearing that he was the boss.

Burt Langdon looked exactly like a male version of the battle-ax Ross had thought Elaine would be their first meeting.

He smiled wryly, admitting that he'd been warned about Burt. Elaine hadn't lied.

Among those in the room were Tom the manager and Bob the tech from The Daddy Club. They both smiled at him, their expression benign. Langdon's, however, was sharp and hard.

"Thank you for giving me your time for this presentation," Ross began.

"I hope Elaine's right, that you actually have something to say," Burt interrupted, with no apology and a lot of belligerence.

Elaine quirked her eyebrow as if to say, "What you see is what you get."

Langdon was obviously a man who was determined to be convinced. No problem, Ross thought, mentally adjusting his emotional shell so that he wouldn't take any barbs to heart. The guy only wanted to be assured that Ross's company had the better deal. That's all Ross wanted to convince him of, so they were already on the same wavelength.

Ross began by giving his company's background, how many years they'd been in business, who their customer base was, what kinds of products they sold and what services they provided as part of any package with RP Computers. He made sure he got everything in before Burt even thought of squirming restlessly in the chair, indicating a too-long presentation.

Ross then made his summation in a series of slides concerning what Data, Ink, needed to accomplish on their project, mostly to show that he understood the requirements thoroughly. Unfortunately, as he talked he found himself all too aware of Elaine in the darkened room. He couldn't see her. He didn't even have to know where she was sitting to have his senses on alert.

It was her perfume.

The damn scent teased his senses, giving him only a minuscule whiff of it every so often but just enough to resurrect visions of the other night. Every time she shifted, it caused the scent to gravitate toward him. Each time it did he remembered her nearly naked against him, her nipples engorged from his ministrations and her hands clawing at him because she could not get enough of what he was doing.

Somehow he kept himself focused on the presentation, although he had no clue how he managed it. Just knowing she was there was making him crazy. When he flipped on the lights again, he looked straight at Elaine. She had an odd smile on her face as if she knew every thought in his head. If she did, he hoped to hell she was having the same ones.

He opened the discussion for a question-and-answer session. Burt, not unexpectedly, hit him first.

"I talked with another company and they used the

same software solution you're proposing," Burt said. "They told me it took nine months to implement. That's way too long. We've got to be up and running in three."

Wonderful, Ross thought. The man went right for picking apart the presentation. This would be fun.

"I don't know what components they were using," Ross replied, "but they couldn't have been this exact solution. Not for a nine-month delay. If they did, my bet would be they didn't have an experienced tech on-site to implement it. This is a fast-start solution, and we provide you with techs on-site for three months to install and implement it. You need a good foundation, which takes time, and then you *will* be successful. But not nine months' worth. We install one module at a time and ensure that it's up and running properly before we move to the next module. That means your accounting group can be working while the sales group module is being installed. That might feel longer, but it's not. It's good installation procedures that keeps a company from total downtime. Otherwise, you guys might as well take a long vacation, because that's about as much work as anyone will get done in the interim."

Burt grunted, noncommittal about the answer. With a guy like this, Ross considered it a victory. The others laughed at his vacation comment.

"You know that's happened," Elaine said cryptically to her boss, who grunted again. Ross had a pretty good idea she was referring to their last dealings with Dall Computers. "It wasn't worth what we saved."

"What company can afford that kind of disruption to their operations?" Ross asked, driving home Elaine's words. "None."

Burt grunted again, then asked pointed questions

about the operating system. He liked another, long-standing one better.

Not only was Burt from the "Show Me" state, he also thought he was a tech expert, something some executives liked to do in these presentations. Ross reassured him the newer system ultimately worked better and fit Data, Ink's needs perfectly.

"If you want to send Bob to school on the system you like, great," Ross said, adding the kicker. "Those techs are few and far between. But you better give him a big raise because he's going to get offers like crazy from other companies who want him on staff."

"Okay," Bob said happily as everyone laughed.

Burt set his jaw in a clear show of nonamusement.

Tom the manager piped in. "I have to tell you, Burt, that Ross has put together a good package for us. He's a creative guy, very creative when it comes to problem solving. Bob will back me up on this. We both went to his Daddy Club, the other night—"

"Daddy Club!" Burt's voice was half astonished and half scornful.

"It's a club for single fathers who need to learn to deal with their kids and the new relationship," Bob added.

"Then why are you there?" Burt asked. "Or did you divorce that pretty thing you married?"

"Who do I look like, Arthur?" Bob asked in wry tones. "They let me in because I'm a new father and ignorant. And desperate. The wife is going back to work."

"I pay you a fortune. What are you doing with it?"

"Paying my mortgage. Becky's a surgical nurse. She loves it, and she needs to keep her hand in."

"Oh."

"It's great," Tom said. "We're having experts on keeping the kids entertained during weekend custody, how to deal with teenagers and Arthur's personal favorite—an attorney to talk about men's rights in a divorce."

"There aren't any," Burt said grimly. "I should know. I'm getting killed in my divorce."

"You've got young kids," Elaine said to him. "Burt, you ought to go to The Daddy Club."

"I don't know," he said, frowning.

"You're the CEO of a big company, and you have kids about the same age as Ross's two children. How involved were you with your older set of kids?"

"What's your point?" Burt asked.

Elaine leaned forward. "I've heard you say a lot that you want to be more involved with your little ones. You've even got toys in your office, for when they come in. But your time is very limited. Ross is a single father with sole custody of his two. He does a balancing act Dr. Spock would envy. Maybe you'd benefit from a few meetings of The Daddy Club."

Ross didn't know whether to kiss her or kill her. If Burt came to a meeting, he would be questioning everything.

"It really looks like a good deal," Tom added. "I have to say I was impressed."

"Okay. When?"

"Next week," Ross said promptly, realizing that if Burt had to wait until the next scheduled meeting he would dismiss it as too long.

"I thought we had a meeting next month," Bob said, innocently.

"No, next week," Ross corrected. He assessed what Elaine had passed over about the ages of Burt's children and added, "It's about building a strong relationship with your kids while working fifty hours a week and going through a divorce."

Burt smiled briefly, but it was a genuine smile. If he knew he was being manipulated a little, he didn't seem to mind. "Okay, I'll try to be there."

Elaine gave Ross a look that said she'd make sure he'd be there.

The meeting closed out pretty much on that note. Ross thanked Burt for his time, the man more congenial than when the presentation had started. Ross especially thanked Bob and Tom, not too much so that the others would notice, but enough for the two to know he appreciated the boost on another level. A level that might just pay off on this one.

When the others left, Elaine hung behind. Ross took her hand, lifted it to his lips and kissed it. "You are a princess."

She laughed. "You were a prince of patience."

"You did warn me about him."

"He just wants the best for his company."

"So do I, and that's RP." He looked at his watch. "You deserve dinner. My mother's got the kids until the store closes, then I have to pick them up. How about dinner out, then we pick up the kids and go to my place?"

"Deal."

Their dinner was an early seating at a good Princeton restaurant, but neither of them minded. Ross felt as if he was on a cloud, and although a little mist under his feet was the only thing supporting him, he wasn't worried. Said feet were well in the door at Data, Ink, and the big boss was coming to a Daddy Club meeting. He asked Elaine about Burt's situation, learning that the man had had a much younger wife who had given him a girl and a boy. Now she wanted out of the marriage, one that had had no prenuptial agreement, giving the lawyers a field day. Basically Burt felt like a fool, and he'd been a bear with everyone ever since. Ross would have his work cut out for him in finding the right thing to impress a man who probably put Arthur in the shade as a chauvinist.

The kids were rambunctious when Ross picked them up at his mother's. Elaine had driven her own car, common sense logistics, but Ross worried that she would veer off at any moment, deciding dinner was more than enough. He wasn't happy until she parked at the curb of his house.

"It's a mess," he warned.

Inside, she looked around the living room. "Some toys out, big deal."

"*My* toys," Ariel said.

"Uh-uh," Jimmy sneered, grabbing up a doll.

"Kippy!" Ariel wailed, running after Jimmy to rescue her favorite doll.

The two raced around the living room before Ross bellowed for them to stop. He hated that Elaine was seeing them at their worst tonight. Ariel snatched her doll away, then took a swing at her brother. She whacked him on the arm. Jimmy hit her right back.

Ariel burst into tears while Jimmy said, "She hit me first."

"Ariel, you know hitting is wrong," Ross said sternly.

"Na-na," Jimmy said to Ariel.

"But he took her doll," Elaine defended. Ariel went over and cried at the feet of her sympathizer.

Ross skipped telling her the reasons the act was indefensible. He knew the real problem was that both kids were tired and needed to go to bed. "Jimmy, stop tormenting your sister. You were wrong, too. Now, before both of you have to sit in the chair for half the night, let's go upstairs and get ready for bed. Say goodnight to Elaine."

"Good night," Ariel said, through sniffles and a hug.

Jimmy said nothing, just raced up the steps.

Ross raised his eyebrows. Normally the kid fought bedtime. Now if only Jimmy's sister would follow suit.

"Ariel, let's go," he said.

"No." She clung to Elaine more tightly.

"Can't she stay up a little while longer?" Elaine asked, clearing having sympathy pains for Ariel.

"No-o-o." Ross drew the word out. He looked at Elaine meaningfully, meaning for her to remember their purpose here. An *adult* drink of celebration. A chat. That was all, in keeping with their agreement to clear business before moving on to pleasure. But he wanted it. Badly.

"Oh."

"Ariel, bedtime. Now."

The child did not give up. "Can 'Laine give me a bath tonight?"

"Only if it's a short bath." Ross felt as though he could concede on one point for Ariel, as long as she didn't take forever in the tub.

"'Kay."

"'Kay," he echoed.

Elaine's eyes widened. "Oh, I couldn't—"

"It's easy," Ross said, taking her by her arm. Ariel held her hand, and they led Elaine up the stairs to the kids' bathroom.

When he saw the mess Jimmy had made, Ross set his jaw. Damn kid had left toothpaste bits in the sink and his dirty underwear on the floor for the last time. Ross had Elaine start the bathwater for Ariel, while he cleaned up after his son for expediency's sake.

"It's too hot!" the child complained after she'd undressed and tried to step in the water. She looked like a mini Venus de Milo, with her little arms wrapped around her torso and her hair flowing past her shoulders.

Ross saw the steam rising and quickly mixed in more cold. He tested it. "There. It's tepid, just the way you like it."

Ariel smiled and climbed in. She started fooling around with her bath toys.

"I'm sorry," Elaine said.

"No problem."

Elaine began to bathe Ariel. She was a little awkward but okay, Ross thought. Ross went back to cleaning up the sink.

A few moments later, a shriek of pain pierced the small room, reverberating off the walls like visible sound waves.

"It's in my eyes! Daddy!"

Ross pushed the dripping shampoo out of his daughter's eyes, quickly soaked a sponge in clean water, then squeezed it out over Ariel's face. He noticed the mild kids' shampoo was in the back of the bottle tray and cursed himself that he didn't think to tell Elaine to use that one rather than the adult one, up front.

"I'm sorry," Elaine repeated.

"It's okay," Ross said, frowning at the way she knelt helplessly next to him. Elaine looked like a frozen popsicle.

He smiled when Ariel pronounced herself better, then chuckled when she added, "You give me a bath, Daddy."

"Okay."

"I'll just go downstairs," Elaine said, getting to her feet.

Ross nodded. "I'll be there in a few minutes."

He spared an extra minute in the bedtime process to read Ariel a poem from one of her books. Reading always settled the child down. He looked in on Jimmy, too, who was playing with his zoom cars. Ross tucked the boy in his car bed. The kid was Jeff Gordon in the making. They talked about bathroom messes and their required punishments for a few minutes before Ross said good-night.

He hustled downstairs. Elaine stood in his living room, looking lost. She also looked like a corporate version of Venus de Milo, one who enticed the man to find the naked, vulnerable creature underneath. He steeled himself from such thoughts.

"I'm really sorry about the bath," Elaine said. "She was screaming and upset. It was awful. I was awful. I'm terrible with kids. How could you let me near her when you're so capable and I'm not—"

"It's okay. Ariel's a pain in the butt at bath time. She knows she's supposed to get the kids' shampoo, but Jimmy's been using mine lately and so the little wench never said a word to you, knowing she'd get away with it." He grinned. "She paid."

"But I should have realized—" She shook her head.

"Don't worry about it, okay?" He wasn't in the mood to discuss shampoos. "Let's have some wine."

"I better go," she announced instead.

"But what about the wine?" he asked, confused.

"I have to drive." She grinned wryly, taking the sting out of her words. But her next sent the message he didn't want to hear just now. "We...we need to be all business, Ross, for your sake."

He wanted to argue, but couldn't. She was being noble for his sake, and who could argue with that? He got her coat and helped her into it. "Thanks for all your help with the presentation."

She smiled. "You helped yourself more than I helped you."

He would save drinks for a full champagne celebration *when* her company signed his up for the contract. He refused to think of *if* and hedge his bets. He'd gained enough ground with Data, Ink, today to deserve the *when*.

Not wanting her to get away with all business, he leaned over and kissed her on the mouth. Her lips were tangy, intoxicating him with their sweetness. He deepened the kiss and met no resistance from her, their tongues melding together as if they'd been kissing all their lives and knew every nuance that gave delight.

Realizing he was crossing a line he shouldn't, he raised his head. "We're still in our business zone."

"Yes." She pressed her fingers to her lips, then smiled slightly. He nearly kissed her again. "We said not until after the contracts have been signed. If we accept RP's offer."

"You will."

She giggled. "You have supreme confidence. I like that."

He hoped so.

Chapter Five

She wasn't a sensible professional. She was a noble idiot.

When she had left him, the night of the presentation, he'd said, "We'll see what the next few weeks will bring. Then we'll talk."

Somehow that aggravated her more than anything on the drive home. And the next day. And the next. She kept telling herself that her mother was right about Ross. Her common sense rolled out how incompetent she was over a simple thing like a bath. Whenever she even thought of cooking an egg, her instinct came to the fore with all sorts of negatives about domestication. Generally, every fiber of her being said that it had been good to walk away that night or she would have wound up in his bed.

So they were business professionals now. Ha! she thought in disgust. Every time she talked with Ross on the telephone, her body melted at the sound of his voice. Her brain remembered images and sensations of being half-naked in his arms. Her heart beat harder at just the thought of him. She missed him terribly. He'd agreed too quickly with her that night for her feminine side.

She wanted to make amends, to show him and herself what he was missing and that a maid and a nanny could take care of the miscellaneous, like bathing kids and running a vacuum. Good intentions mixed with bad until Elaine needed a certain kind of reaction from Ross, just to show that he found her irresistible.

They were in a funny kind of waiting game, and she was almost ready to burst from it. She had to know if Ross was, too.

She wasn't scheduled to see Ross for a business meeting anytime soon, but she knew where she could find him most early evenings. With that in mind, she dressed carefully and then went out shopping for a hammer and a croissant.

Ariel and Jimmy were at the store with their grandmother, waiting for Ross to pick them up. Ariel didn't run to greet her, clearly not trusting Elaine to return the hug without something getting hurt. But the little girl smiled around her thumb as she sat in a chair. Feeling naked under Ruth Naomi's shrewd gaze, Elaine quickly buttoned up her coat over her low-cut, V-neck sweater.

"How you doing?" Ruth N. asked. She nudged Jimmy who knelt in a chair behind the counter so he could see above the top.

"May I help you?" Jimmy intoned solemnly.

Elaine blinked, taken aback by the boy's seriousness, then said, "Yes, I came to buy a hammer."

"Claw, sledge, tack or ball peen?"

Elaine gaped at the choices. "I don't know."

"Grandma," Jimmy whispered loudly. "I don't know what to say when they say they don't know."

"Ask what she wants it for."

Oh, Lord, Elaine thought, scrambling to come up

with some answer that showed a smidgen of intelligence regarding hammers.

"What do you want it for?" Jimmy intoned again.

"Ah...to hang a picture?"

Jimmy smiled in relief. "That's a claw hammer. You could use a ball peen, too, but you can't take a nail out with a ball peen hammer if you make a mistake."

"Wow," Elaine said, impressed. "You sure know your hammers, Jimmy."

He smiled happily. "Yeah."

"The kid's got the store in my will," Ruth N. commented proudly.

"Whaddo I get, Grandma?" Ariel asked from the depths behind the counter.

"A big kiss and your college tuition."

"I like the kiss."

Ruth Naomi bent down and kissed her granddaughter. "I thought you would."

Elaine chuckled.

"You get the hammer over there," Jimmy said, pointing to an aisle.

"James, you *help* the lady find the hammer."

Elaine spun around at the deep voice that already sent shivers of anticipation up her spine. Ross smiled at her, deepening the grooves in his lean face. He looked good in a dark suit, pale-yellow shirt and striped tie.

"Do I hafta?" Jimmy whined, either unwilling to give up his perch which his sister could then take, or unwilling to help Elaine because he didn't like her.

Elaine hoped it was the perch and not her but she doubted it.

"You're the hardware guy," Ross said. "Helping people find what they need is the job, son."

"Why don't *you* be the hardware guy for Jimmy?" Ruth Naomi suggested. Her eyes gleamed with mischief.

"Yeah, Dad. You be the hardware guy."

Yeah, Dad, Elaine thought. *Be the hardware guy.*

Her mental message must have reached him. "Okay, I'm the hardware guy."

"There's a thrill, Elaine," Ruth N. said.

Elaine grinned. She could feel how goofy the grin was, but she couldn't get it straightened out into one of wry amusement. Ross was a hardware guy all right. His mother had no idea.

Ross led her to the aisle and down it. The lane went nearly to the open area for the workshops. None was in progress tonight, and Elaine could barely see the coffee bar beyond. Maybe if she couldn't see it at her angle, they couldn't see her and Ross at theirs.

"What to you need the hammer for?" Ross asked, stopping by a pegboard display of hammers.

"To hang a picture." Elaine stared at the hammers, realizing she could hurt herself in eighteen different ways with the things.

She remembered her real purpose was to see if Ross was dying from their self-imposed moratorium on a relationship. She unbuttoned her coat, revealing the secret weapons.

Ross's gaze moved right on target. He stared at her low-cut sweater, the upper curves of breasts enhanced by her push-up bra. Elaine knew she ought to be ashamed of herself, a professional businesswoman acting like a teenager in front of him.

"I'll hang the picture," he said, in a voice that cracked.

Elaine smiled, very pleased with his reaction. She

fanned her face and chest. "That's very nice of you, but I really should buy a hammer. Is it hot in here or is it me?"

"You, definitely...." He paused. "It's warm. How about a drink at the coffee bar?"

"That would be nice."

He looked down the empty aisle toward the counter area that wasn't visible. "The kids are playing hardware helper with Mom. Let's go."

He escorted her over to the Muffins section of the store, hammers of any sort forgotten. She didn't say a word about the two coffees he ordered. Obviously he was oblivious to what cooled down a body. She sat opposite him at a tiny table for two and slid her coat off her arms. He watched her, not saying a word. Her foot bumped his leg under the cramped table.

"I'm sorry," she said automatically, then cursed herself for missing an opportunity.

"It's nice of you to come here for a hammer," he said.

"I like to give my business to people I know," she replied, casually maneuvering her foot around to find his leg again. She caressed the table pole instead. Sighing in disgust, she added, "I still can't get over how well your presentation went the other day."

"It didn't seem that way at first," he replied, sipping his coffee.

He shed his jacket. The muscles of his arms and shoulders shifted smoothly under his shirt as he moved. Elaine watched, fascinated with how the male body worked.

"Anything said at Data, Ink?" he asked.

She heard the words but they took a minute to register. "Oh. Yes. Burt is definitely coming to your meeting."

Ross cursed. "I have to do something really impressive."

She wanted to tell him he was impressive enough as it was, but he wasn't talking about himself. "That wouldn't hurt."

She maneuvered her foot again, just very casually adjusting herself in her chair. Naturally one's foot would sort of swing with the movement...this time she connected with something other than the table's one central leg. She didn't apologize and she didn't move her foot out of the way.

Ross's eyes widened when she rubbed the inner side of her foot against the back of his calf. His hands with the coffee cup shook slightly.

Elaine smiled. "I was wondering, Ross..."

"Yes?" He snapped out the word abruptly, clearly disturbed by what she was doing.

"How is your company in supplying notebook computers?" she finished, rubbing her foot harder against his leg.

"I...ah...I... Hell, yes. What are you doing?"

"We're looking at upgrading our reps' portable equipment late next year. It's just talk right now, but it could happen."

"No problem. Whatever you want." He swallowed a gulp of coffee. "Dammit, Elaine, what *are* you doing?"

Elaine stopped her foot. "I'm sorry."

"I'm not. You look terrific. You smell terrific. You're making me crazy. What *are* you doing?"

She grinned and sipped her coffee. The liquid had cooled to tepid and it slid down her throat in one smooth swallow. "I think I'm flirting. I hope you don't mind."

"Hell, no." He grinned in return. "You keep doing that, and we're not going to make it until after the contract's signed."

She laughed. "At least I know I can do something domestic."

"What's that mean?"

"Nothing. Just nothing."

"MIC, JUST ACT like a foundering father."

Micah looked at Ross in exasperation. "Okay, but what's a foundering father? Do I sign a declaration of dependence?"

"If you have to. Look, just talk up your child and your wife or something. Decide if you're separated or divorced."

"Divorced." Micah grinned.

"And you need help with domestic things and your kid. It's not rocket science."

"But you called it a foundering father."

His brother was being obtuse, something Micah managed very well.

Suddenly Micah roared with laughter. He slapped Ross on the back. "Don't sweat it, big guy. I'll give the performance of a lifetime."

"Hell, don't do that!" Ross exclaimed, envisioning Micah going way over the top as a helpless father in front of Burt Langdon.

"You wound me. Look, I know how to play to the audience," Micah said. "I adjust, don't I? I've adjusted to a downward swing in my career, haven't I? I can't believe I'm reduced to doing Noah Siedelman's bar mitzvah."

"Noah's dad owns half of downtown Philadelphia, Mic," Ross reminded his brother. "That's hardly downward to give a private performance. It's like David Cassidy coming to play at your college graduation, which he did."

"I feel like David Cassidy sometimes," Micah muttered.

Ross knew the professional rock gigs for his brother were coming farther and farther between. Mic was facing the real world and not liking it.

"Just sit in on The Daddy Club tonight, Mic," Ross said. "Act like an upper management dad who has to juggle work and kids. If Burt Langdon likes what he sees tonight, he'll have to be very favorable to my abilities with his company's business. If RP gets that contract, I'll be set for a long time to come and so will Jimmy and Ariel. You want that, don't you?"

"God, but you manipulate the guilt almost as well as Mom does," Micah complained. He grinned and slapped Ross on the back. "No problem."

"Just call me Rauol."

"Hell, no. Just be Micah."

He clued in his mother and her friends that Micah was playing a part tonight for the special Daddy Club meeting with Burt Langdon.

To his delight, not only did Tom, Bob, Clark and the infamous Arthur come to the meeting, but four more did, as well. One of them wasn't even from Data, Ink, and he wasn't Micah in disguise. George had stopped in the hardware store and had seen a flyer advertising the meeting. He was a divorced father of three girls who lived five hours away. Ross promised himself he'd do a long-distance father workshop for the guy.

Burt came in the door, bringing the feeling of a hurricane with him. It wasn't so much that he walked in as that he strode with such energy and purpose that the air stirred constantly around him. Elaine entered behind him, looking terrific in a pants suit.

He needed a subdued Elaine tonight, one who would not distract him from the meeting. When she looked at him, a special smile didn't play at the corners of her mouth. Instead, her gaze was clearly anxious. He knew his must be, too.

He made introductions all around. Micah, the only one in a T-shirt, one that screamed the lyrics to Led Zeppelin's "Stairway To Heaven," clearly wanted to see who had the stronger handshake grip.

He grasped Burt's hand lustily, pumping it up and down. "Good to meet you, man. I'm in upper management, the wife's a horror and I love my kids. How about you?"

Before Ross could intervene in the disaster about to happen, Ruth Naomi wedged herself between Micah and Burt. She looked the CEO in the eye and said, "It's a pleasure to meet you, Mr. Langdon. I'm Ruth Naomi Steadwell, Ross's mother, and I own the store here. Take your time, look around, buy a few croissants, a couple of saw blades and some coffee. We have African beans as well as South American."

Burt smiled at Ruth N., a genuine smile of pleasure as he shook her hand. "You are a very clever woman, Mrs. Steadwell. I admire your ingenuity with this store."

Ruth N. arched an eyebrow, looking young and flirtatious. "I am a very unique woman, Mr. Langdon, and call me Ruth Naomi. All my friends do."

"Will we be friends?" Burt asked, not letting go of her hand.

"I doubt I'm in your league for more than that," Ross's mother replied.

"I would think differently."

Ross stared at his mother, realizing he was witnessing sexual attraction between man and woman. But the woman was *his* mother. She took care of the problem in her own special way.

"How old are your children?" she asked.

"I have two grown children from my first marriage," Burt said. "And two little ones, about the ages of those two."

He nodded to Jimmy and Ariel.

Ruth N. gave him a gimlet stare. "Took yourself a trophy wife the second time around, eh?"

Ross choked at his mother's audacity. He looked in panic to Elaine, who looked back, stricken. The group went deathly quiet.

Burt gave back Ruth Naomi's gimlet stare. "You've got a lot of nerve."

"And common sense," Ruth N. shot back. She patted his hand. "Now you know why I'm out of your league, honey."

Burt roared with laughter. He raised Ruth N.'s hand to his mouth and kissed the back of it in surrender.

To distract himself from the thought of his mother and Burt together the way he wanted to be together with Elaine, Ross turned to Micah. He said nothing, just glared at his brother, who suddenly remembered himself and thereafter toned down the George Carlin routine. Ross shuddered, hoping his brother hadn't given himself away. Burt had looked nonplussed—but whether from Micah's greeting or Ruth N.'s performance he didn't know.

"Good luck," Elaine whispered at their only opportunity to speak.

"Thanks." Ross wanted to kiss her and nearly did, the temptation urging him to say the hell with everything and just go for it. He intended to, but in its time and place.

"Did you see that between Burt and your mom?" she asked. "I think it's cute."

"You would." Ross shuddered again. "My mother amazes me."

"Burt amazes me. Just keep doing what you're doing."

"And I'd better do it now," he said, knowing he should start the meeting.

After he got everyone seated, Elaine in the coffee bar with the rest of the "observers," he explained the purpose of The Daddy Club, for Burt and the new members. He then turned it over to the former CEO of RP Computers, Ralph Premigin, who had lost a daughter and son-in-law in a boating accident over ten years ago and had become guardian to his young granddaughters. A widower, he had had to run a company and raise the two girls by himself. He was now semi-retired and the granddaughters were about to enter college.

Burt leaned forward, listening intently. Ross leaned back, satisfied that he had connected two men with a mutual interest in something unrelated to the proposal his company was making. And yet whatever Ralph said would reflect well with Burt's perception of RP Computers, a very good thing.

He hoped he hadn't been so clever that the subtlety would get lost in the talk.

"So you're saying to me that a man can't run his

company properly *and* have time for his children,''
Burt interrupted, when Ralph pointed out the two were
a conflict in priority. ''You've let your company suffer.''

''No. I've delegated a lot of what I used to do to my
vice presidents and managers, like Ross here,'' Ralph
said. ''Yes, my company's probably more top heavy
than others, but RP Computers has grown 25 percent
in sales and 20 percent in profits since I've done so.
Not only do I have time for my kids, but I've got a
better company for it. What's your priority, Burt?''

''Both.'' He frowned. ''I've got two sets of kids, one
grown and one young. I wish now that I spent more
time with my first.''

Ross could feel his eyebrows shooting up in surprise.
For as tough as Burt had been in the presentation, he
had a tender side. The business side of Ross was
tempted to tap into that by making a connection between his children and Burt's. Ross put the notion back
in the Pandora's box where it belonged. His company
was the best for the project, and he didn't need an
underhanded trick to get Burt to his way of thinking.

''Then your first priority is to your children,'' Ralph
said, drawing back Ross's attention. ''But right now
you're saying the words, not meaning them. You know
how I started? I made it an absolute point to take my
kids to lunch every Friday. I made sure no appoint-
ments were scheduled, no meetings that could run overtime into the lunch. I worked everything around that
Friday lunch. Pretty soon it wasn't a hassle. Then it
was great. You got an hour a week for your kids, Burt?
Don't tell me you can't find it.''

Ross smothered a grin at his boss's hard edge. He
looked over at Elaine whose eyes were wide, expecting

an explosion. So were the rest of the guys from Data, Ink. Micah opened his mouth to say something stupid, and Ross glared him down. Only the new guy who had come in off the street was nodding his head in agreement.

Burt thrust his jaw forward, then said, "Hell, Ralph, I could do it if Melinda would let me. She's being hard-nosed about visits."

"When's that divorce lawyer coming?" Arthur asked eagerly. "I told you we needed one."

"Next meeting," Ross replied.

Even Burt chuckled at the promise. The workshop ended shortly after that. Jimmy and Ariel came over to him, both giving him a hug. Ross was surprised at the sudden affection until he saw his mother's smug expression. Ruth N. had prompted them…and he was grateful. A little exploiting never hurt anyone. He had a feeling his mother was the exploitable one.

Sure enough, Burt made a beeline right for her. She introduced him to her friends, all of whom flirted with him. Ruth Naomi then took him on a tour of the hardware store, Jimmy and Ariel tagging along.

"Oh, Lordy," Elaine said, coming up to stand next to him.

"My words exactly. Now what do I do?"

"Just let it go." She grinned. "Your mother could charm the birds out of the trees."

"My mother would hit them over the head with a sledgehammer to get them down."

"How'd I do?" Micah asked, bouncing up to them.

"You were spectacular," Ross said. "Don't do it again."

Micah chuckled. "Boo on you, pal."

"Seriously, Mic, thanks for helping out." Ross

meant it. Once his brother had settled in, he'd been fine and the needed body to fill out The Daddy Club roster.

Ruth N. came up to them. "Burt's not a bad guy, just misguided."

"Don't make it your mission in life to save him, Mom," Ross warned, fearing the implications.

"Take Elaine home, honey. I'll take the kids with me tonight."

Ross eyed his mother, wondering if he could hit her over the head for her blatancy. He wanted nothing more than to say to hell with everything and make love to Elaine. When he glanced over at Elaine, he saw the same naked longing in her gaze.

"Go," his mother said.

Ross and Elaine were still grinning ruefully when they left the hardware store.

"I guess we've been told," she said, not quite looking at him.

"I guess so."

Ross tried to seem outwardly casual. Inside, his anticipation level shot up ten thousand points. The last time they were at her house…and the kids were at his mother's tonight. It wasn't going to happen, however.

"I better go," she said, confirming his thoughts.

As he walked her to her car, Elaine didn't act anything but calm and oblivious, while Ross thought he'd explode with frustration. He'd have another lonely night in his bed.

And it was lonely. The moment he walked into the house, it was lonely. He wondered if Elaine felt the same as he.

Ross set his jaw. He turned and walked out of his house and drove to Elaine's.

When he pulled in front of her town house, she already had the door open. He didn't have to say a word, just walked inside and kicked the door shut. She came into his embrace, and he kissed her, all the pent-up need finding an outlet from which he wouldn't turn back.

She melted against him, her tongue swirling with his. Her fingers plowed through his hair, her nails lightly raking his scalp. Her mouth was already feverish and demanding, as if she'd had the same exact thoughts as he. As if she'd had to screw up her courage to get him here and now didn't intend to let him go. She shouldn't have worried. He'd lie down like a lamb for her.

Their coats were an effective barrier. Ross slid his hands underneath hers and found her body. He cupped her derriere, kneading the flesh under her thin wool trousers. The soft mounds gave under his palms as he worked them. She moaned in the back of her throat, even as the kiss deepened. He thought only of getting closer to her, of fulfilling all the frustrations of the past week, even though they both had excess baggage. It didn't matter for this one time.

Her coat hit the floor to lie in a puddle at her feet, even as she unbuttoned and pushed his from his shoulders to join hers.

He eased his mouth from hers, to string kisses down her neck and minister intently to the sensitive spot just behind her earlobe.

"We're lousy professionals," she murmured, sagging into him.

He lifted her against his burgeoning flesh. "I want you, Elaine. I could tell you a hundred reasons why I should be strong but I don't give a damn about those things. Send me home now."

She chuckled against his ear, then nipped it sweetly.

"Forget it. I can't walk away, either. Maybe I've been too decisive all my life, but will you stay?"

"Hell, yes." He kissed her again until her mouth was swollen with it and her eyes half-lidded and her body pressing to his so tightly they couldn't have wedged a sheet of paper between them.

She took him by his shirtfront and led him out of the small foyer. He thought she was taking him to the living room, but she bypassed that, and they went straight into her bedroom.

The room was small and cozy, with all sorts of pictures and wall hangings. The bed had piles of pillows against its headboard, as well as piles of books on the nightstand next to it. All the implications washed through him for a split second and while each had a place, nothing mattered except Elaine and what she meant to him.

She turned and faced him. He didn't give her a moment to speak, to hesitate, but pulled her straight down on the bed.

They bounced once, the water mattress undulating under them. Ross burst into laughter at the unexpected movement. Elaine melted against him, giggling.

"Hey, if you're going to sleep alone, you might as well enjoy it," she admitted ruefully.

He pushed her hair back from her face and kissed her, the amusement still on both their lips. Then the full force of their restrained attraction rose to the surface like a wellspring bursting through the last of the earth. The kiss deepened, and they reached for each other's clothes. In the back of Ross's mind, he realized he felt no awkwardness, no vague guilt. He only wanted to show Elaine how much he cared for her.

Her sweater came off easily, and as he wrestled free

the front hook of her bra, her breasts spilled into his hands. Her flesh was hot and silky, her nipples hardened points. He rubbed his thumbs against them, feeling them distended even more at his touch.

Elaine got his shirt opened, then brought her breasts to his chest. He felt them burning his skin, her nipples tickling his chest hairs. He buried his face in her shoulder, breathing in the scent of spring flowers and woman. Her skin was so soft and so tangy that he thought he would die from it. He never wanted to surface from this moment again.

Ross lifted his head, kissed her forehead, her eyelids, her cheeks and her lips, then dipped lower and laved his tongue around the curves of her breasts. Elaine's hands flexed on his shoulders as she moved restlessly under his ministrations. He finally took one nipple in his mouth, suckling and nipping at the tender flesh. Elaine moaned, her fingers clawing at his shoulders, her need clearly as intense as his own.

Ross gave her other breast the same careful attention, finding the movement of his tongue that sent her spinning over the edge of self-control.

"Ross, Ross," she murmured, his name a litany.

Pure pleasure seeped through him as well as a desire to please her so thoroughly his name would be the only one she would ever utter the way she had just now. His own need pressed him unbearably, but he channeled it to a far corner of his mind. Elaine kissed him and clawed at him, becoming more frantic. Her hands were a cool fire on his skin. She touched him everywhere.

Suddenly he couldn't shed the rest of her clothes fast enough. Her long legs were like smooth satin, firm and slender. Her woman's flesh was hot and moist, the folds giving to his caresses. Elaine's fingers worked his belt buckle open and she pushed his clothes off him, her hands stroking him. It had been so long and he was afraid he'd embarrass himself like a schoolboy. But he refused to leave her unfulfilled.

Elaine tensed, then moaned his name as her body took release. Ross smiled against her breast, feeling the pulsations of her flesh even as she panted his name so deliciously again. He rolled her onto her back and poised himself against her, ready to plunge in.

Myriad emotions flashed across his brain. Not only hadn't he made love in a long time, but she was the first since— He didn't want to finish the thought.

What if he disappointed her? What kind of complications would intimacy cause for their working relationship? A million reasons not to make love, and yet one that overrode them all. This was Elaine.

He took a deep breath and filled her with himself. She accepted him fully. He held for a moment as she wrapped her arms and legs around him, cradling him inside herself. They moved together, each thrust heightening the last until Ross heard her cry out his name again. His release came a heartbeat later, taking him into dark, sweet, sweet oblivion, different and better than ever before.

He held Elaine tightly, feeling skin to skin, intimate flesh to intimate flesh and knew an appreciation that nothing could mar.

Ross grinned.

Chapter Six

Surfacing from a sleep that left her limbs like lead, Elaine felt a heavy pressure on her chest. Disoriented, she opened one eye to find the first gray haze of dawn trying to push past her bedroom curtains. The heaviness on her chest didn't ease. In fact, it was joined by a hot weight half on, half off her.

And the sound of snoring in her ear.

The night rushed back at her as she turned her head. Her nose smacked against another of its kind. The physical pain was nothing.

"Oh, God," she said out loud.

Ross snorted. In the bare light she could see his eyes flutter open. They closed, then opened wider this time, as events clearly rushed back to him.

She could feel his nakedness against her nakedness. She'd wanted this. In fact, she'd arranged it, knew she would the moment she was aware that his children would be spending the night at their grandmother's. She'd even sensed Ruth Naomi helping her, on some sort of conscious level, to have Ross be with her for the night.

She wouldn't have traded it for anything.

The moment she realized it, she grinned. Ross relaxed and smiled.

"I thought I was seeing some regret," he said.

"Eventually," she replied. "You'll have it, too."

"I will?"

"You won't?"

He thought for a moment, then snuggled closer. "Well, hell. Especially if I don't get Data, Ink's account."

"That's one regret we hope we don't have," she said, then chuckled wryly. "If only Burt could see me now. I'd be fired."

"No," Ross said.

"Yes." She made a face. "He's a prude about intercompany relationships, especially when there are negotiations involved. He likes them to be very uncomplicated."

"We tried our best."

"Yes," she agreed. "We did."

Lovemaking with Ross couldn't have been better. The sensations he made her feel. The way his voice sent shivers down her spine every time he whispered something to her. The incredible intimacy. She'd never quite experienced that before. They should have kept to their bargain, not to further their relationship until a decision had been made about the project. But she didn't regret failing this time. Not one damn bit.

Still, she had personal baggage she'd never discussed with him. She hadn't told him about her two marriages. At first, when they'd talked about his situation they hadn't been involved with each other, and then she'd never seen an opportunity to tell him her own past after that. He'd never asked about her, either.

"I'm going to have to go soon," he said. "Mom

will be bringing the kids home to get changed. Jimmy's got school. I don't want to explain my not being there. Or worse, have my mother explain it. God knows what she'd tell them.''

Elaine giggled, thinking of the endless possibilities of Ruth Naomi's excuses. Then she sobered and turned away. ''Ross, I need to tell you… Remember I said I wasn't good with children? I'm not so good with men, either. I've been married twice before.''

To his credit he didn't pull away from her. She glanced over at him. He was still staring her way.

''Twice?'' he echoed.

''Well, yes.'' She nodded. ''I know it's a hell of a time to tell you—''

''No kidding.''

Hearing the sarcasm in his voice, she stopped. ''I understand.''

''No. No. I'm mad at myself for never asking about your life, especially when I haven't shut up about mine.''

''That was okay,'' she assured him. ''I was very interested, believe me.''

''And that's my point. I should have been just as interested.'' He kissed her cheek. ''Can you forgive me?''

She relaxed. ''I'm just glad you're okay with it.''

''Right.''

Something in his tone had her gazing intently at him. In fact she turned her body to really get a look at his face. ''Ross? You're not okay with it.''

''I…it's a shock. What happened?''

''I married the first time when I was in college. It was a classic case of mistaking infatuation with love. We both realized it quickly enough. The second…well, it was another classic case of thinking compatible interests make the marriage. He was an executive with an insurance company. We were more friends than in love, which I found out when he had an affair.'' She swallowed, needing a pause. ''I told you I was lousy with domestic things.''

''You did well with Ariel. And you're doing great with me.''

The approval sent her spiraling with pleasure. She kissed him on the mouth. ''Thank you.''

They lay together for a little while longer, watching the sun slowly lighten her curtain. Elaine knew she had many reasons why they shouldn't have given in to their attraction, but she was content. She wouldn't ask for more than this. Truly, she didn't have a right to.

''I have to go,'' he said finally.

She nodded, not speaking.

He kissed her gently, then slipped from her bed. She watched him pick up his clothes and walk naked into her bathroom. He was pure male, latent muscle, fine dark hairs, flat stomach and well-defined arms. Sighing with pleasure, she wondered how a man could look so good in the morning.

One domestic thing she could do well was coffee. Elaine got herself up and wrapped a pretty, flowered, thigh-length robe around her. She groaned with rueful satisfaction, her muscles protesting movement while she walked to her kitchen.

She set up her coffeemaker with the proper ingredients and at the proper levels, then stood and listened to it whoosh water through the cycle. Instead, she heard her front door lock turn and her door open. She froze.

''Elaine, honey, you better get up for work!''

Elaine's eyes widened, and her limbs loosened from

their panic. She raced on bare feet out into her hallway to find her mother in the open front door, about to set a bag on the foyer floor.

"Mom!" She clutched her robe at her breasts and the junction of her thighs even knowing it wouldn't keep out maternal X-ray vision. "What are you doing here?"

Her mother smiled, clearly not noticing anything untoward. "Oh, you're up. Aren't you freezing in that little robe? I came over with your dinners for next week now because your dad and I are leaving for the retail outlets down in Rehobeth Beach in a few minutes. It takes three hours to get there…"

Her mom's voice trailed away at the distinct sound of a door opening upstairs. She looked at Elaine's coat on the floor, then at the other coat on the floor. Her mother then looked up the steps. Finally she looked at Elaine.

"Elaine?" Ross's voice boomed like a hydrogen bomb through the little town house.

"Down here." Elaine stared at her mother pointedly, then called out, "My mom's here!"

"Your mom—!"

Mary glared at her. Elaine shrugged, although she only wanted to crawl back into bed and pull the covers over her head.

Ross came downstairs. He smiled at Mary Baransky. "Good morning. Ah, there's my coat." He bent down and picked up both coats, hanging Elaine's over the newel post. He looked at Elaine. "I…ah…"

She realized his dilemma. "Don't even think of being Sir Lancelot and staying. You've got the kids to take care of—"

"Omigod!" her mother exclaimed. "You left those little children at home alone for...for sex!"

"He's not stupid, Mom," Elaine replied. "Of course he didn't. They spent the night at their grandmother's."

"She would have a field day with this. Mrs. Baransky, let me explain..." Ross began, hell-bent on being Sir Lancelot anyway.

Elaine cut him off. "Ross, I will see you later."

He raised his eyebrows, dubious about leaving her. "You sure?"

"Very."

He nodded and took his escape, putting his coat on as he did.

Elaine heard him shut the door behind him before she faced her mother. Mary Baransky looked ready to slice and dice her.

Ross CALLED HER late in the afternoon from his cell phone. Elaine snatched up her phone when Tina put the call through.

"Hi, how are you?" he asked.

She smiled at his deep voice. "Okay."

"I hated deserting you with your mom. I hated leaving, period. Are you sure you're okay?"

"I'm fine, truly." She chuckled at his worry, pleased that he did worry about her.

"What did your mom say? I got back in time so mine has no suspicions about where I was."

She burst out laughing. "Ross, you sound like a teenager."

"I feel like one."

Elaine's face heated, but from sheer pleasure not from embarrassment. "So do I."

"So what *did* Mom say?"

She wondered how to express her mom's feelings without offending him. Probably she shouldn't say anything at all, but she couldn't help griping just a little. "She likes you and she thinks I'm all wrong for you because I can't cook an egg."

Ross chuckled. "You're not that bad, are you?"

"I am. You know why she was there that early? Because she was dropping off my dinners for the week. I can't cook at all."

"Surely you're exaggerating." He tried to console her.

"Ross, honestly I'm not."

"Tell you what. Jimmy needs a new coat, so we have to go to the mall tonight. His got torn somehow at school, a mystery that has yet to be solved. Afterward the kids and I'll come over and help you cook your own dinner."

"Really?" She thought of all the possible disasters that could take place, but couldn't resist being with Ross. Maybe this time she would get lucky.

"Sure, and I'll check out your microwave."

"Okay."

Tina poked her head in as soon as Elaine hung up the phone. "So what did the hunk want?"

Elaine smiled happily. "He's cooking me dinner tonight."

Tina narrowed her eyes. "Aha! You *are* different today. Did you and Ross—?"

Elaine broke in before her assistant could finish her questions. "Tina, do you want to get fired?"

"Nope, not me," Tina replied with earnest tones. As she shut the door behind her, she was heard to say, "So you did!"

"Damn!"

Elaine laid her head down on her desk for a moment. If Tina could see the growing intimacy between Ross and herself, then so could others. Maybe even Burt could see the change in her. The last thing Ross needed was a tag of collusion being attached to his proposal. Burt was scrupulous about business and personal relationships. She and Ross were going to have to talk.

WHEN HE ARRIVED with his children that evening, she thought she was in control of her emotions. As he stepped over her threshold, he could have been a rock star. She felt all her bones melt and her mouth gape open. Her body wanted to throw itself at him, and she had no clue how she held herself back.

"Hi, lady!" Ariel said, happily throwing her little arms around Elaine's thighs.

Elaine staggered with the force of the child's enthusiasm, then patted Ariel on the back. "Hi, Ariel! How are you today?"

"I'm vewwy good," Ariel announced, before letting go of Elaine. The kid popped her thumb in her mouth.

See? Ross mouthed to her, grinning broadly.

"Hi, Jimmy," Elaine said, noting the boy hanging back. "How are you? Did you get a new coat?"

"How'd you know?" he demanded, looking grim as if she were an intruder.

"Oh…your dad told me. He said you tore yours at school."

The boy rounded on his father. "Dad! Why'd you tell her that?"

"It made for good press? What's wrong with Elaine knowing?" Ross asked. "Unless there's something you haven't told me about how the coat got ruined."

Jimmy clammed up.

"You can watch some television," Elaine offered the boy. "It's in the living room."

Jimmy brightened and raced off for the other room. Ariel followed more slowly.

Ross frowned. "Although it isn't their hour for TV, I guess I won't worry about it...."

Stepped in it again, Elaine thought, realizing she'd made yet another parenting faux pas.

"It'll keep them busy while we fix dinner. Since we're alone..." He stepped over to her and kissed her on the mouth, a small, tender, gentle one. "Now on to the kitchen."

Elaine led the way to the back of her town house, conscious of his gaze on her. She hoped he liked what he saw.

"Got a small pan? And an egg and some milk?" he asked, after settling his coat on a chair. At her nod he continued. "I'm going to show you that you *can* make an egg." He walked to the cooktop and motioned her over.

"First of all, don't turn the heat up too high."

She stood next to him on the counter and followed his directions. In minutes she'd made fluffy scrambled eggs. Elaine couldn't decide which was more impressive—the eggs or the man next to her.

From the living room she could hear Jimmy and Ariel giggling at cartoons.

Suddenly she realized she liked the noise in her house, the coziness of other humans interacting with her. Ross and his family filled the rooms in a wonderful way that she'd never realized had been missing.

That was dangerous, she admitted. Very dangerous.

"So how was the dinner *you* cooked?"

Ross smiled in amusement as Elaine grinned. They

were cleaning up the dishes together.

"Not bad for anyone else, and terrific for me," she said. "With your help."

"You did most of the work."

"Yeah, I did, didn't I? I had no clue you could add eggs and bread in a casserole thing like that."

"A frittata," Ross said, giving her the correct name for the meal.

"No wonder you're the president of The Daddy Club," Elaine said.

"And a client, too."

"Wait'll I tell my mom I made dinner for four almost all by myself. She won't believe I actually cooked an egg. I should have gotten the camcorder out."

"Hey, if you tell yourself enough times you can't do something, you'll be sure you *won't* do something."

"Ah, the philosophy lesson of the day."

He leaned over and kissed her cheek. "You just need confidence."

In the bedroom she was a tigress, meeting him every step of the way. In the kitchen, she was a little mouse, scared of her shadow. He liked helping her. It appalled him to think her mother still brought dinners over every week. Elaine truly couldn't be that undomestic.

He thought about her revelation of two former marriages and had to admit the odds of making a good marriage were against her. *Two.* Her explanations for both were logical, however. He knew plenty of people who plunged into situations without seeing the overall implications. In a way he was glad he hadn't known, because it would have colored his initial attraction to her. Now he knew her, knew the type of person she was, and he couldn't see the reasons for either marriage dissolving as being her fault.

Still, they were rushing headlong into a relationship he wasn't sure he was ready for.

"Ross?"

He turned to her. "Yes?"

She looked away, cleared her throat, then looked back. "I think we need to talk about last night."

"I know," he said.

"I think we've gotten ahead of ourselves."

"I think you're right."

"And I think we have the proposal to take care of first. Burt has a real old-fashioned idea of inter-company relationships, especially when it concerns giving business to someone an employee's involved with. I don't want that to blow up in your face."

"I can see your point." She was right in both cases. He knew it last night when they made love. He also knew it this morning when he woke up with her in his arms. He just hated hearing her say it out loud. "You're saying we need to wait and in the meantime be friends."

She nodded.

"It's just for the duration, right?" he asked. "Just until Data, Ink, awards the contract. Or do you really want to end what's happening between us for good?"

"Do you?" she asked.

He gazed at her, trying to see behind her concerned expression to how she was truly feeling. It had been a long time since he had walked down this road of dating or relationships or whatever this was with Elaine. He didn't know the etiquette. He didn't want to scare her off. He wasn't ready to commit himself.

To hell with it, he thought. He'd tell her how he felt,

and if he got hurt, he'd learn for next time. Or rather there would be no next time. He wasn't going through emotional pain again, having had more than his fair share already.

"I only want to be friends in the short term," he said finally. "In the long term, I'm going to want more. That's how I feel now."

Her breath came out in such a relieved rush there was no mistaking it for anything else. "That's exactly how I feel."

He grinned, then reached for her and kissed her thoroughly. Their mouths blended with latent heat. When he eased his lips away, his head was spinning and he was ready to march her right upstairs again. "We can't do that for awhile now."

"I know," she murmured.

"I wish you didn't."

She chuckled and relaxed against him. He held her for a long moment, content. Finally he said, "So now what?"

"I don't know."

He still didn't know days later, but he decided he was having fun. He and the kids went over and helped Elaine cook her own dinners until even Jimmy was warming to her. Ariel just loved Elaine, always happy to see her. Personally he couldn't keep his hands off her. Even now, as they walked through the mall, window shopping, he put his arm around her and pulled her close for a few seconds while the kids stepped into the toy store.

"You know that's dangerous," she murmured, when his hand dipped a little lower on her spine.

"No one's behind us in the aisle," he replied, then looked behind them to make sure. "Yep, all alone."

"Is this going to be a Daddy Club lecture?" she asked. "How to grope a woman while in the toy store with your kids?"

Ross grinned at her. "It'd be a great one."

"I have to tell you, my mother is getting a little annoyed that I'm learning to cook." She smiled, incredibly pleased with herself.

Ross smiled back. "Maybe I ought to start a women's club."

"I think they already have those, to get away from cooking and housework."

"Daddy, Daddy! Look!" Ariel shouted, pointing to a shelf. "A Magic Waterbaby! I want one, I want one."

"A what?" Elaine asked.

Ross explained the kiddie phenomenon. "It's a baby seal that turns colors in the bathtub."

"How neat," Elaine said. "Here, Ariel. I'll buy it for you. Jimmy, what do you want?"

Ross frowned, watching his kids race off to grab their chosen toys. He didn't approve of giving in to the kids' on-the-spot whims; they would never learn discipline that way. Neither was it the way for Elaine to win their friendship. But Elaine's excited expression stopped him from protesting. After she paid for the toys, Jimmy getting a micro racing car set, they all resumed their stroll through the mall.

"Elaine, I don't think it's wise to buy the kids gifts just because they see something they like," Ross began, feeling he needed to head off any other ideas she might get.

"But I'm happy to do it," Elaine said. "And the store clerk said those seals are becoming all the rage. He said they'd be the toy everyone stands in line for at Christmas. Ariel won't have to worry that 'Santa'—'' she tweaked his nose, ''—can't find one for her.''

''Maybe so, and I appreciate that,'' he said. ''But the kids have to learn they can't get everything they want when they want it. That's not good.''

''Oh, I understand that,'' she assured him.

''Okay,'' he said, relieved. In truth, he wanted the kids to like her for her. He wanted to banish the notion that she was terrible at things domestic.

He also wanted Elaine back in his bed. Now. Friendship ate dirt, as far as he was concerned. Now all he needed were a few little corrections in Elaine's thinking, a few culinary lessons and an accepted proposal.

Piece of cake.

Chapter Seven

She was on a roll.

Okay, so she was on a *platonic* roll, Elaine admitted ruefully. Still, she was having a wonderful time just being with Ross and his children. Ariel truly liked her, and Jimmy seemed to like her a little. She wasn't asking for more than that.

But she felt as though she needed something to put her over the top with the kids.

Tina walked into her office with a sheaf of papers. "Fan mail from the boss."

Elaine groaned. More Burt memos. She wished Ariel was there to draw on them again. That would be a nice touch. "What are they about?"

"The usual. Our monthly sales figures are down once again."

"Oh, no," she muttered. "He'll be pressing all of us now. If Ross can undercut Dall Computers on this new bid, then we can show a better profit margin. That'll calm Burt down."

"For a little while," Tina added, making a face.

After Tina left, Elaine could feel her own face screwing up in a permanent grimace of frustration. Burt would be hell to live with, if the figures didn't come back up. But perhaps Ross's company could offer more in services to offset Dall's low prices. Many companies today were willing to spend extra to get more. Maybe she could work something with Burt to give Ross a better chance.

But what to do about Ross's kids?

An idea, so brilliant that it mentally blinded her, hit in the middle of the afternoon. She called Ross immediately.

"I want to take the kids to the ballet," she said. "And you. To *The Nutcracker*."

"Sure you don't want another hockey game?" he asked in return.

"Don't tell me you're a macho man."

"Ah…" His voice trailed away over the telephone line.

She laughed. "You can suffer for one night."

"I really don't think the kids are ballet material."

"That's just because they haven't been to one. Have they?"

"No. Never."

"Good. They'll like it." Elaine grinned. "My mother took me when I was their age, and I just loved it. For years afterward I took dance lessons."

"That's you. My kids…I don't know. I'm afraid they'll get antsy."

"That's why we'll see *The Nutcracker*. It's great for kids. And perfect for the holidays. I'll get the tickets."

To her pleasure, she did. Several evenings later, Elaine was very content as she parked her car in an evening parking garage. Ross sat next to her, and the kids were in the back. She felt as if she had a family. *This* family. Domestic life had suddenly opened up a path for her, and she was running down it. Happily.

Tonight would be so special, she thought. Something she would always treasure. Maybe even look upon as a turning point for herself. She would show she had competence with children, at least. This could be the thing that broke her kid jinx.

As they walked up the Avenue of the Arts in Philadelphia's Center City to the theater, Ross took her hand and she he squeezed it. Little Ariel took her other hand, naturally, freely, and grinned up at her. On Ross's other side, Jimmy held his dad's free hand. Elaine's heart filled with such emotion that she knew it would burst. Many places they passed had their Christmas decorations up, giving the city a warm feeling. Perfect, she thought. Everything was working out perfectly.

When they reached the theater, she shepherded her guests down a side aisle of the Philadelphia Center for the Performing Arts. The beautiful new building, part of the city's renaissance, was rapidly packing in a sell-out crowd. It was overwhelming, and the kids were feeling it a little bit. Ariel, in front, wasn't quite with the program any longer.

"Go on, Ariel," Elaine said, nudging the reluctant child who stopped at the opening to their row.

Ariel didn't move, her body against Elaine's legs, as she stared at the grumbling people rising to allow them to pass.

"Dad, this is stupid!" Jimmy announced loudly from behind Elaine.

"It's a treat from Elaine, so knock it off," Ross told him, then added from the back of their little line, "Elaine, come on."

"Ariel won't move." Elaine realized she probably

should have gone into the row first, but Ariel hadn't hesitated until a moment ago.

Still, her idea to bring the kids to a top-flight production of *The Nutcracker* was a good one. The ballet was excellent, the story one even kids could grasp, and it was something they'd never done before. Ross hadn't sounded enthusiastic, but just some edges needed smoothing out—like who walks first into the row. Elaine felt the ballet was something she could handle as an event, better than cooking and other domestic doings. She took many a client to performances just like this one, and so knew the ins and outs.

The house lights suddenly blinked their warning three times, plunging the hall into near darkness before coming back on.

Ariel screamed.

Ross let out a sigh loud enough for the people around them to hear. He tried to reach beyond Jimmy and Elaine to get to his distraught daughter, but failed. "Pick her up, Elaine."

Elaine tried to pick Ariel, who was now beginning to cry, but the child's coat was bulky and Ariel kept slipping through her arms. "Ariel! Stop crying."

Ariel wailed louder.

"Is she going to cry like that all night?" an exasperated person demanded.

"I'm sorry," Elaine apologized. "The lights scared her."

She gripped Ariel harder this time, finally lifting the child into her arms. Ariel's weight was unexpected, and Elaine staggered against a man who yelped when she stepped on his toes. "Sorry."

Ariel hugged her, pressed her face against Elaine's neck.

Elaine patted her on the back, while she got them both over to their seats in the middle of the row. She bent to set Ariel in the seat, but the child's weight once again carried her farther than Elaine expected. The child cried a little more when her head bumped the back metal rim. Elaine sat next to Ariel and fussed with the tiny buttons of the kid's coat, trying to undo them. Ariel pulled away.

"There, there. It's okay now. Isn't this nice?" She added the last brightly to both Jimmy and Ross.

"It stinks," Jimmy announced, flopping into his seat.

Ross leaned over the boy and Elaine. To Ariel, he said, "Are you okay, honey?"

"No," Ariel said, then stuck her thumb in her mouth.

Elaine sighed with relief at the child's abrupt silence. "See? She's fine, Ross. Sit down. The ballet's about to start."

"I'm missing *Nick at Nite,*" Jimmy informed them.

"What did we talk about, son?" Ross asked, his voice no-nonsense.

"Well, I am." Jimmy just stared ahead at the closed curtains.

Clearly he and Ross had some agreement about behavior. Elaine realized the child wasn't enthusiastic. Well he would be, she thought, when the ballet started. Everything was just new and different, a little more sophisticated than Jimmy was used to. That was all that was troubling him just now. He'd like the fight scene with the Mouse King. Any boy would want to fight a mouse.

The house lights went down for a final time. Ariel's whine revved up as the orchestra did. Elaine panicked.

"Look!" she said, pointing to the stage as the lights went on there and the curtains parted.

Ariel looked as the dancers pirouetted onto the stage, graceful and polished. "I have to go to the potty."

Elaine blinked, not sure she heard right. "The potty? Now?"

"Now."

From the other side of her, she heard Jimmy say, "This is dumb."

"Now," Ariel said, with more emphasis.

Ross turned to her.

"What's wrong?"

"She has to go to the bathroom," Elaine whispered. "I'll take her."

"I don't know..." he began, dubious.

Ariel got off her chair and proceeded to go the long way down the row, people shuffling to let her pass. The kid showed not an ounce of fear this time, heading unerringly for the aisle and the center's rest rooms. Elaine hurried after her, causing a jack-in-the-box effect as patrons rose one at a time to allow her to pass them, then sat down again.

She finally caught up with Ariel near the end of the row. "Wait for me."

"Okay."

Only Ariel didn't. Elaine leaped past the last two people in their row and raced after Ariel, who headed for the orchestra pit with unerring accuracy. Elaine finally snagged the child and turned her around. She spotted Ross half-standing, clearly ready to come after them. She waved him back down, hoping he could see her gesture in the dark, then frog-marched Ariel up the aisle to the ladies room.

Elaine let out a huge sigh. "Here we are."

Ariel stuck her thumb in her mouth but otherwise didn't move.

Elaine frowned. "Go ahead. You can go to the potty now."

Ariel didn't move.

"You said you had to go," Elaine reminded her. "Do you?"

Ariel nodded.

Elaine opened a door to a free stall. "Here."

Ariel only looked at her.

Eventually, Elaine realized the child wanted something more from her. "Do you need my help?"

Ariel smiled around her thumb.

"Oh, boy," Elaine muttered, but managed the job.

The usher was reluctant to let them back down to their seats before intermission, but Elaine knew Ross would come looking for them if they didn't show up soon. She promised the usher they would be quiet as mice going back to their seats—and they were. Ariel was a little angel about the whole thing.

Elaine sat with satisfaction. Ross leaned toward her. "Everything okay?"

"Perfect," she said, smiling and settling in for the performance.

"And it was perfect. The kids sat quietly, watching the stage and Elaine began to believe this had been a great idea. For five minutes. Until Ariel popped her thumb out of her mouth and spoke into the darkness. "Potty."

Elaine groaned.

"I gotta go. Now."

NOBODY SAID TOO MUCH the rest of the way back to Hardware and Muffins, where Ross had left his car.

Ross wasn't sure whether the silence was a blessing or not after the disastrous night. He was ready to hog-tie his kids and ready to tell Elaine next time he'd pick the children's entertainment.

When they reached their destination, his mother, clearly having waited for their return, came out of the store. Ross got out of Elaine's car, and Ruth Naomi leaned down and said through the open passenger door, "Come in and have some coffee, guys."

"Yeah!" Jimmy cheered. "I get to eat finally."

Ariel chose that moment to wake up. "Hi, Grandma. I saw the nut!"

"That's my girl," Ruth N. said approvingly. To them all, she added, "Come on in. Margie and I were just shooting the breeze before cleaning up. We've got some leftover pig's ears that have to be eaten or tossed. Help us out."

"I can't," Elaine began reluctantly.

Ross couldn't let her go home feeling the way he knew she did. "Come in, please."

She looked at him, while the kids got out of the back seat and went with their grandmother into the hardware store. At last she turned the key, killing the engine.

"All right. I could use coffee."

He went around the car and opened her door for her, then ushered her inside his mother's store. They went down the aisle in silence, this time more contrite, to the coffee bar area.

Jimmy and Ariel were already picking out their treats. They each had cups of milk in front of them.

"Look!" Ariel exclaimed, holding up her plate with two hands. "I got a piggy ear, Daddy."

"That'll keep her up all night," he said, after fussing over his daughter's snack with great appreciation.

"Hey, Dad, can we take home some of these for tomorrow?" Jimmy asked, pointing to several lonely muffins left in the display case.

"Fifty cents each," Ruth N. bargained.

"Sheesh! They're stale, Mom. You can't sell them tomorrow anyway."

"Don't bet on it."

Elaine chuckled. "Okay, I'll take one. Better the bargain now than the broken tooth tomorrow."

"You have a point."

Ross bought the muffins Jimmy wanted and coffee for himself and Elaine. The first sip of the sharp, rich, bittersweet liquid put a genuine smile on her face, as the four of them sat at the counter.

"I think I'm getting addicted to the coffee here," Elaine said.

He reached over and stroked her free hand. "Good. Keep feeding your addiction."

The deflated expression lifted from her gaze, but she said, "I don't know, Ross. I really made a mess of it tonight."

"No, you didn't. I should have sat on the two of them."

Ruth N. leaned over the counter and said, "So how was the ballet?"

"Ariel liked the rest rooms better," Elaine told her with a straight face.

Ross burst out laughing.

His mother cocked an eyebrow. "That bad, eh? Well, they need some culture in their lives." To her granddaughter, she said, "Ariel, honey, how did you like the dancing toys tonight?"

"Pretty!" Ariel pronounced around a mouthful of pastry.

"All the Christmas decorations were neat," Jimmy said. "Can we go back sometime to see them again?"

Elaine gaped at the two kids, while Ross laughed again, more ruefully this time.

"I'd say the little rug rats got some culture out of the evening after all," Ruth Naomi said to Margie, who tweaked Ariel's nose.

"Kids are always a surprise," Ross admitted.

"Did you really like the ballet?" Elaine asked Jimmy.

He made a face. "Yuck! Just the Christmas decorations, but I guess if I hadda go to the stinky ballet to see them, I would. But not all the time."

"Okay," Ruth said. "So his culture is more materialistically oriented, but it's a start."

"You thought the lady dancers were pretty?" Elaine asked Ariel, to Ross's amusement.

Ariel nodded, too intent on her pig's ear to answer with speech.

"Just don't ask her not to go to the bathroom forty-thousand times during the performance," Ross advised.

"I figured that out myself." Elaine grinned at him.

"Ballet is tough on macho boys and fidgety little girls," Ruth N. said.

"That's a long time to ask them to sit still," Margie added. "But it sounds like you did okay."

Elaine's mouthful of coffee came flying out as she sputtered in disbelief at that assessment. "'Okay'! Oh, God."

Everyone rushed for napkins to clean up the mess.

"Do that again," Jimmy said, delighted with the faux pas.

"I think you just made a major Brownie point with

Play TIC-TAC-TOE and get FREE GIFTS!

HOW TO PLAY:

1. Play the tic-tac-toe scratch-off game at the right for your FREE BOOKS and FREE GIFT!

2. Send back this card and you'll receive TWO brand-new Harlequin American Romance® novels. These books have a cover price of $3.99 each in the U.S. and $4.50 each in Canada, but they are yours to keep absolutely free.

3. There's no catch. You're under no obligation to buy anything. We charge nothing — ZERO — for your first shipment. And you don't have to make any minimum number of purchases — not even one!

4. The fact is, thousands of readers enjoy receiving books by mail from the Harlequin Reader Service® months before they're available in stores. They like the convenience of home delivery, and they love our discount prices!

5. We hope that after receiving your free books you'll want to remain a subscriber. But the choice is yours — to continue or cancel, any time at all! So why not take us up on our invitation, with no risk of any kind. You'll be glad you did!

YOURS FREE
A FABULOUS MYSTERY GIFT!

**We can't tell you what it is...
but we're sure you'll like it!**

A FREE GIFT —
just for playing

TIC-TAC-TOE!

The Harlequin Reader Service® — Here's how it works:

Accepting your 2 free books and gift places you under no obligation to buy anything. You may keep the books and gift and return the shipping statement marked "cancel." If you do not cancel, about a month later we'll send you 4 additional novels and bill you just $3.34 each in the U.S., or $3.71 each in Canada, plus 25¢ delivery per book and applicable taxes if any.* That's the complete price and — compared to the cover price of $3.99 in the U.S. and $4.50 in Canada — it's quite a bargain! You may cancel at any time, but if you choose to continue, every month we'll send you 4 more books, which you may either purchase at the discount price or return to us and cancel your subscription.

*Terms and prices subject to change without notice. Sales tax applicable in N.Y. Canadian residents will be charged applicable provincial taxes and GST.

If offer card is missing write to: Harlequin Reader Service, 3010 Walden Ave., P.O. Box 1867, Buffalo, NY 14240-1867

BUSINESS REPLY MAIL

FIRST-CLASS MAIL   PERMIT NO. 717   BUFFALO, NY

POSTAGE WILL BE PAID BY ADDRESSEE

HARLEQUIN READER SERVICE
3010 WALDEN AVE
PO BOX 1867
BUFFALO NY 14240-9952

NO POSTAGE
NECESSARY
IF MAILED
IN THE
UNITED STATES

my grandson,'' Ruth Naomi said, grinning at Elaine after they took care of her ''spill.''

''I'm on a roll tonight.'' Elaine lifted her cup for a fresh sip of coffee. This one stayed where it was supposed to.

''Aww,'' Jimmy groaned, disappointed.

''Come on, guys. Finish up your milk so Grandma and Margie can close the store,'' Ross said.

The kids, tired, didn't dawdle through their snack. When he and Elaine finished theirs, he walked her out to her car. The street was nearly deserted, so he took a minute to lean her against her driver's side door. Her body melded to his, delightfully enticing his senses.

He kissed her, their tongues mating almost dreamily together. He tasted coffee, sharp and bittersweet, on her lips. She sighed when he finally released her.

''Thank you for putting up with my children this evening,'' he said gravely, holding both her hands.

She chuckled. ''Good Lord, but they almost liked it.''

''It was a noble gesture on your part. I'll kill them when I get them home.''

''Oh, no. Don't punish them. It was my fault for taking them to something too adult.''

''Even so, they need to behave properly. They know they're supposed to.'' Ross pressed his lips together, then said, ''Don't worry, I won't totally shred them.''

''That doesn't make me feel any better. I think they're actually starting to like me.''

''They do like you.''

''Ariel does. Maybe.''

''No *maybe*s. Jimmy, too.'' He knew his son. If he didn't like Elaine he would have acted up even more than he had.

"Next time the zoo?"

"That'll work."

He kissed her goodbye again, although he was very reluctant to let her go. When he heard the jingle of the Hardware and Muffins front door, he finally released her.

"You know the last thing I want is for you to go home without me," he said in a low voice, his mouth against her ear.

"Great minds think alike." She sighed and gently pushed him away. "But thinking and doing are two different things."

He chuckled and opened her car door for her. She slid onto the seat, tucking her legs in gracefully.

He leaned his head in the doorway, but didn't kiss her. "Drive safely."

"You do the same."

"I will."

He eased the door shut and motioned for her to lock it. She pressed the power locks and they clicked satisfyingly. He stepped around to the sidewalk and watched her drive off, then turned to see his mother and children by his car. He went over to them.

Ruth Naomi smiled. "Feeling good, I'll bet."

"Yeah," he agreed, although he knew he should be annoyed with his mother's matchmaking overtures.

"Well, you deserve to. Here are your rug rats, ready to go home and go to bed."

"Did you kiss Elaine?" Jimmy asked, making a face.

"Yeah, I did. She was very nice to all of us tonight, and I at wanted to show I appreciated her efforts to give us a big trip."

"I don't have to kiss her, do I?"

"I don't think so," Ross mused while his mother smothered a chuckle. "A thank you would be nice. After all, you liked the decorations. How about we call her tomorrow and you do that. It'll get you less time-out."

"Okay." The boy didn't sound too unhappy about it.

"I say 'thank you,'" Ariel told her father.

"Yes, you will, my girl." He unlocked and opened the backdoor of his car. "Everybody in, please. It's Sandman time."

"Sing the song," Ariel demanded of her father, while he belted her into her seat. He dutifully sang the first bars of "Mr. Sandman," her favorite bedtime lullaby.

"All those voice lessons with Mr. Pierre and you sell computers," his mother said. "You coulda been a star."

"I could have been Micah," he reminded her.

"Oh, yeah. Okay, so you're the responsible one. I like that."

Ross laughed and kissed his mother on the cheek. "I'll see you tomorrow, Mom."

"I'll be here." She paused. "Just one word of advice. Better wrap Elaine up now."

"I'm working on it."

Chapter Eight

His kiss could take her breath from her body. His mouth was rich chocolate. His body was a hard wall of muscle. One touch and she wanted him.

Naked, he was a god—

"Elaine."

Elaine jerked herself out of her reverie and stared at her boss, Burt Langdon. The weekly conference was the usual mixed bag of promises and frustrations on the production front. She'd sat through hundreds, so it was no wonder she'd zoned out.

"Yes, Burt?"

Burt's sharp gaze bore into hers. "What do you think?"

She tried to look innocent and knew she failed. "I would tell you, but I'm not sure what we're talking about here."

Burt's eyes narrowed. "We were talking about the bids we've received on our new information systems."

Elaine eyed him. "I may not know what we're talking about, but I know we *weren't* talking about that."

Burt suddenly grinned. "Actually I was asking for more coffee for everyone."

"Sugar, no cream."

Everyone chuckled. Elaine sighed with relief that she truly hadn't missed anything in the meeting.

After it was over, she went up to Burt, deliberately waiting until everyone else was out of the room.

"I'm sorry I was daydreaming there for a moment," she said.

"Good thing I like you."

She smiled. "Thank God you like me."

"Just don't make it a habit," he said, adding, "Hell, I know these meetings aren't getting us anywhere at the moment, but we've got to have some kind of reporting continuity. I like putting everyone on the hot seat. You're the only one who gets away with it. You tell it to me like it is, not what you think I want to hear."

She remembered the first time she faced this man, all hard business, and told him his idea for a project was unworkable, expensive and just plain wasteful of everyone's time. She just couldn't keep her mouth shut on something that was detrimental to the company, no matter where the idea originated. He had glared at her, through her, dressed her down for her views and then thanked her for telling him her honest opinion. She'd gone rubbery in the legs from the immense relief shooting through her that she still had a job. After five years, Burt still managed to instill the same fear in her as he had that day.

"Burt, can I ask you something more personal?" she began, reluctantly. "What sorts of things do you do with your children?"

"What? When we're together for the weekend?"

She nodded.

A funny expression crossed his features. "I didn't

used to know, but that Daddy Club I went to actually helped.''

Elaine smiled broadly, so pleased to hear he thought the meeting he attended had been worth his time. ''See? I told you.''

''Don't push your luck,'' he said. ''Mike Felderfield wants your job.''

Elaine realized he wasn't kidding. A threat was typical Burt maneuvering. He always liked to keep his managers on their toes. ''Mike couldn't do the job I do.''

''Mike doesn't doze off at meetings.''

''I didn't doze off. I lost focus for one minute while we discussed our network systems analysis for the tenth time—''

''Aha!'' He tapped her arm in a friendly gesture. ''I knew you weren't totally out of it.''

''Gee, thanks. So what do you do with your kids for entertainment? Would you take them to the ballet?''

''What are you, nuts?'' he asked rhetorically.

Confirmation of her idiocy, Elaine thought wryly. ''I guess I am because I did take some kids and it wasn't a great success.''

''Next time try the amusement park or a kiddie movie. Even then you have to be careful. One movie Vannessa loved, Tony didn't. He whined through the entire thing until I was ready to lock him in the car, I was so disgusted with him.'' He hooted with laughter. ''The ballet! That's rich.''

''I think I need The Daddy Club,'' Elaine muttered.

Suddenly the idea had merit. Hadn't Ross formed it to help fathers find their way with their children? If she wanted to develop a domestic side and lose her children's curse, then the club should be able to help her, too.

"Can I ask you a question?" Burt said, sobering.

"Sure."

"That woman, Ruth Naomi. Is she with someone?"

Burt actually looked vulnerable, which was a frightening thought. Elaine wanted to lie but knew she wouldn't. "Not that I'm aware."

She said nothing else, giving him a chance to share or not as he chose.

Burt only nodded and said nothing more.

As they went their separate ways, she tried to imagine Burt and Ruth Naomi together. The image eluded her, for which she was eternally grateful. For as long as she'd known Burt, she knew he'd been married to a woman barely older than herself. Trophy wife was the term, and Burt was now paying for it. Ruth N., on the other hand, was as hardheaded as he. *Match* wasn't the word for anything between them. *Brawl* was.

Elaine shuddered. At least her notion of attending The Daddy Club as a client had great merit. She was so enthused that she sat in the front row on the night of the meeting.

"Hi, Elaine," Tom said, coming into the back lecture area. "You waiting for Ross?"

"No." She smiled. "I'm here for the meeting."

Bob, arriving, overheard her. "You?"

She nodded. "I need help with children."

"But you don't have any."

"That's true, but I don't do well with them so I think I need help."

"But..." Tom paused. "But this is a *Daddy* club."

"There are Mommy clubs," Bob said, "aren't there?"

"Oh, I don't know." Elaine shrugged.

"What the hell are you doing here?" Arthur asked, when he spotted her.

"She's coming to The Daddy Club," Tom told him.

Arthur pointed to the coffee bar. "Sit over there with the rest of the women."

"No, Arthur. I'm here as a client," Elaine replied.

Arthur blinked. "What? Like the hair ad?"

She laughed, relaxing a little. The hostility she felt from the men was really a surprise. "Yes, like the hair ad."

Burt came down an aisle with Ruth Naomi escorting him. The two were smiling and chuckling together.

"I bet you say that to all the old ladies," Ruth N. told him.

"Never. You are hardly old."

Ruth N. waved her hand in front of her nose as if to ward off a bad spell. "Good thing you've got money, honey, because you never would have gotten that trophy wife of yours with the BS you're spewing here."

Elaine groaned, horrified at the woman's audacity.

"Hell, I'm out of practice," Burt said. He turned to Elaine. "Hey, what are you doing here? Did something come up at the office I need to know about?"

"No," Elaine began.

Arthur broke in. "She's here as a *client*."

"What?"

"I'm joining The Daddy Club," Elaine said, her voice trailing away as she sensed a wave of negativity roll over her. "Or maybe not."

"That's a great idea!" Ruth N. exclaimed, coming over to her and patting her on the shoulder. "This club needs a woman's perspective."

"No, it doesn't," Arthur said. "We're here to get

away from women's perspectives. We're sick to death of women dumping their perspectives all over us. If she stays, I— Hell, I can't walk. She's in upper management.''

"Don't worry," Elaine said. "I promise I won't hold it against you."

Ross came into the workshop area. He grinned when he saw Elaine. "Hi. I didn't expect to see you here tonight."

"She's joining The Daddy Club," Ruth N. said brightly.

Ross's pleasure faded. "Joining?"

Elaine's self-confidence vanished. Lamely she said, "I thought it would be good to learn how to do things with kids. In case I wanted to do something else with…kids."

Ross chuckled, catching her drift. "Okay."

"You're not letting her stay, are you?" Arthur the chauvinist asked.

"I don't have a problem with that," Ross said.

Ruth Naomi plunked herself into a chair next to Elaine. "Good. I'll stay, too."

"Like hell," Ross exclaimed. He jerked his thumb in the direction of the coffee bar. "The Daddy Club is off-limits to mothers. You're a mother if I ever saw one. Beat it, Mom."

"Good thing you said that with affection," Ruth N. grumbled, getting out of her chair. "You pay double tonight for coffee and muffins, my lad."

"Gladly." Ross sighed with clear relief as his mother left The Daddy Club for the women's oasis at the coffee bar. Her friends, led by Ula Mae, consoled her, mostly with laughter at her getting tossed from the men's environs.

As the males all sat down, others filtering in for The Daddy Club, Elaine suddenly felt conspicuously female, alien to the proceedings. Men looked at her askance, or worse, as if she were about to pop half-naked out of a cake.

Ross called the meeting to order. The last few guys settled in as he said, "Tonight we're going to talk about how to handle the other women in our lives, especially when they're unhappy with our relationship with the children. Anybody have any thoughts on that?"

"Take 'em out and shoot 'em?" Arthur suggested.

The men laughed. Elaine could only wonder at their sick brand of humor. She piped up. "That's hardly helpful, Arthur."

"You'd be surprised," he retorted as men laughed again.

"Arthur's just kidding around," Ross said.

"It's not very respectful," Elaine replied.

"Wanna bet?" Arthur commented.

"Enough," Ross said. "Seriously, does anyone want to start off our discussion?"

No one opened his mouth. Elaine frowned. Granted it wasn't the topic she'd hoped for at the meeting, and granted Arthur had shredded it before it started, but surely it ought to be of interest to the men. That was all they ever moaned about at work, their wives and significant others always complaining that they never do enough at home.

"No one's got anything to say about it?" Ross asked.

"Bob. You've got a new baby. I know you want to help out all you can, that's why you're here. How do you feel when your wife complains about the time you can't devote to your child?"

Bob shrugged.

"Tom? How about you?"

"Not much, just that she wants more help."

"Okay. How?"

Ross looked so wonderful up there, Elaine thought, admiring the way his casual sweater clung to his torso. His jeans were tight fitting, outlining the muscles of his thighs. She decided, when he shifted, that he had a cute butt. When he faced forward, she nearly passed out, her gaze riveted to his bulge.

Ross suddenly coughed, distracting her. She glanced up at his face. It was red and his gaze was pointed at her, reminding her they weren't alone. Elaine realized she'd been caught out staring and had made him too aware of the sexual tension between them.

As she tried to concentrate on a discussion that was as painful as pulling teeth, she knew she'd made another mistake. The Daddy Club wasn't comfortable with her there. Neither was she comfortable being there. The topic was useless to her tonight, anyway.

Instead, she found herself becoming mesmerized with Ross. He was incredibly sexy and his voice sent shudders of remembrance of him in her bed. She wanted him so badly that an urge nearly overwhelmed her to get up, go to him, kiss him senseless and drag him back to her bedroom. To hell with Burt and the others. How she stayed seated, she didn't know.

When the meeting finally ended—early, however, according to the time allowed—she sighed with relief, although she would miss the delicious torture of watching Ross move and breathe. Talk about a sex symbol, she thought. The man symbolized sex for her.

Burt made a beeline for Ruth Naomi, his face lighting up with animation when he reached her.

Ross came up to Elaine and stood at her side. His gaze was on his mother and her newfound "friend." "I think we should be worried about this. God knows, my mother can offend in seven different ways without even trying."

"So can Burt," Elaine replied, frowning as her boss found some reason to touch Ruth N.'s arm.

"Watching my mother flirt is enough to kill the libido," Ross added.

"I hope not," Elaine muttered.

"I like that."

When she turned he was grinning at her. She grinned back.

"My mother has to be ten years older than he is."

"Burt's nearly seventy."

"My mother has to be ten months older than he is." Ross sighed. "How will Burt react if she rejects him outright?"

"I don't know. He's human. Once in a while, this past year when his marriage fell apart, he occasionally killed the messenger."

"Great."

"I'm really surprised, though. He's gravitated to younger women for years, even before his marriage."

Ross looked at her, his eyes narrowing. "Did he gravitate to you?"

"No. That's a policy he's never violated for himself. I would suspect that if he were ever that interested in a woman who worked for him, he'd get her a job in another company before he'd take her out on a date. He's pretty scrupulous."

"Just checking. Shall we go over and break that up?"

"Not a bad idea."

The older people were laughing uproariously when they arrived at the coffee bar. Ruth Naomi was telling a story about "the girls" and their forays to Atlantic City.

"Honest. I truly thought it was Elvis. Of course, it being three in the morning might have been a factor. But this guy was a dead ringer for him as he should be now."

"I still think it was Elvis," Ula Mae said firmly, folding her arms over her chest.

"And you tried to pick him up to prove it."

"Well, a hunka, hunka burning love would be worth it at my age."

"You lead an interesting life, Ruth," Burt said. "Is there room in it for someone else?"

"If you're Elvis, you're in," Ruth Naomi quipped. "Literally."

"Geez, Mom," Ross complained at the sexual innuendo. He and Elaine sat down at a nearby table, close enough to join in the conversation.

"Elaine, you're not coming to another Daddy Club meeting," Burt told her.

"Probably not," Elaine agreed. "Even though the word sexist comes to mind. You guys were no help, anyway."

"What were you doing there, honey?" Ula Mae asked.

"I thought I would learn how to entertain children," she explained, feeling their intense scrutiny.

As one, every woman in the group leaned back and said, "Ahhh."

Family To Be

They all gazed at Ross.

Ross raised an eyebrow, but said nothing.

Elaine turned bright red. Her face was so hot, she thought she would spontaneously combust. Knowing her reaction was silly, she pulled herself together and just said, "I'm not too old to have a child."

"Whooooaaa!" the group exclaimed as a whole.

"What!" Burt exploded, glaring at her. "Are you having a baby, Elaine?"

"If I were, it wouldn't be your business beyond my medical plan," she told him, and cursed herself for her inadvertent words.

"She's got you there," Ruth Naomi said. "I, however, would have questions."

"Why?" Burt asked.

"Well..." Ula Mae began.

"Because my mother likes Elaine," Ross broke in before something untoward could be said. "We all like Elaine, and I'm sure all the ladies would be concerned if she were having a baby by herself. Although it is nobody's business but Elaine's."

"And the father's," Margie pointed out.

"And the father's," the damn Greek chorus repeated.

"Of which there isn't one," Elaine said, quashing all talk about parenthood. She hoped.

"Well said," Ruth N. pronounced. "Men are like little kids..."

That started a whole new discussion about men. This time Burt and Ross were in the hot seat. Her boss seemed to enjoy the sparring, although whenever the subject got to wives, she tensed, waiting for someone to say something stupid to Burt. Ruth N. took her shots, but Burt seemed to thrive on it as if Ross's mother were flirting with him. Ross stayed more in the background and just backed Burt up. Her boss, more than anything, was lonely. He probably had no desire to go back to an empty penthouse.

Elaine understood exactly how he felt.

ROSS MADE SURE he walked Elaine out to her car. He'd been hoping Burt would leave first, so he wouldn't have to hide his interest in Elaine. The man was glued to Ruth Naomi. Instead, he'd had to go the gentleman's route, ensuring Elaine's safety during the eight feet between Hardware and Muffins' front door and her vehicle.

"Thanks for coming tonight," he said. "The cause was noble."

She started laughing. "You like me. You really like me."

"Of course *I* do," he said, pulling her coat collar closer around her throat so the chilly November night couldn't penetrate. "You understand about the guys, don't you? They don't mean to insult you, but they have enough trouble talking about things that make them look inadequate without the enemy sitting in. Men *hate* to look inadequate in front of women."

"You're so in touch with your feminine side," Elaine told him.

"Wanna bet?" Ross growled, pulling her close. Elaine melted against him.

"I'd say I'd stand corrected, but I can't. Stand that is." She smiled dreamily.

"Just so we've got that straight. Why don't you come over tomorrow for dinner?"

"Sure the kids won't mind having klutzoid in the house?"

"They'll love it, especially if you put it that way to them. Come here, klutzoid. I want a kiss."

He lowered his head, about to kiss her senseless, when the jangle of a shop door opening brought him to awareness.

He straightened quickly, Elaine finding her legs suddenly steady as well. They turned to see Burt, his coat on, at the door, talking with Ross's mother.

"I better go," Elaine said.

Ross nodded, not moving as she walked around her car. "Good night, Elaine. Thanks for coming."

"Good night, Ross."

He waved to her as she drove off, then said goodnight to Burt who passed him on the way to his own car.

When he reentered Hardware and Muffins, his mother was waiting for him.

"The man asked me out to dinner."

"Great," Ross muttered. "What did you say?"

Ruth N. eyed him sourly. "You keep acting like I'm Typhoid Mary about to shred your whole business with Burt's company with one sneeze. I'm not an idiot, you know."

"God forbid I should ever say so, Mom. But nothing's been decided and that guy *is* the company. What he says goes. If I'm nervous, I can't help it. So what did you say?"

"Lectures on common sense from my child," Ruth N. muttered. "What the hell is the world coming to?"

"I'm thirty-five now. I can finally read those romance novels Micah and I used to sneak from your nightstand."

"Smart ass. All right, all right." She shrugged. "I

turned him down. I told him I wasn't ready to date yet.''

Ross caught his sigh of relief before it totally got out into the open. "I appreciate it, Mom."

She made a face. "Well, don't. I didn't do it for your benefit. The guy has major baggage right now. He's feeling as if he's made a mistake with a trophy wife and so he's going in the opposite direction for a woman. It's not a thing I want to get caught up in."

"Common sense from one's mother," Ross replied. "You don't suppose we're both growing up, do you?"

"Heaven forbid."

He hugged her, grateful she was his mom.

When he released her, Ruth Naomi said, "Watch yourself with Elaine. I think Burt's wondering what's going on between you two."

"We know." He grimaced. "We're trying."

"Don't try too hard. She's a nice girl and you deserve a little love in your life."

He grinned. "Thanks."

"Just keep her from taking the kids to the ballet." Ruth Naomi shuddered. "Between that and you having Micah watch the kids tonight, Jimmy and Ariel are getting a dose."

The next night, Ross was pleased to see his kids greet Elaine like an old friend. Clearly, neither held the ballet against her. Elaine grinned happily as Ariel dragged her into the living room to look at her preschool drawings. Jimmy showed her his new micro car, then went off to play with it, but his gesture was enough.

"My daddy's cooking 'getties for dinner," Ariel announced after Elaine duly admired the cat and dog and

cow that looked exactly like blobs of brown, brown
and black.

"I like spaghetti," Elaine said. "Maybe your daddy
needs help with the dinner."

"You two could set the table," Ross offered.

"I think I can manage that without a disaster."

As Ross checked his sauce, which was bubbling too
much, and his water pot, which wasn't boiling at all
yet, he listened to the conversation between Ariel and
Elaine as they did table-setting duty.

"You're apposed ta put the napkin right in the middle of the plate," Ariel said. "Jimmy forgets if he don't
see it."

"Really?"

"And ya put the plate right here." Ariel smacked
down the plate with a force of ten. Or so it seemed. In
reality, the heavy stoneware got away from her little
hands.

"Not that hard," Ross warned.

"Tell you what," Elaine said. "I'll put the plate
down. You do the forks and knives."

"I get a knife this time!" Ariel exclaimed happily.

Ross vowed to quietly remove the thing before his
daughter carved herself instead of her meal.

It was *very* nice to have Elaine at the kitchen table
with them, a cozy time that felt…whole. Ross smiled
to himself at the thought. His mother might be dodging
excess baggage, but he was shedding his slowly and
surely. Even the kids looked on Elaine favorably.
Granted, Ariel always had, but even Jimmy chatted
with her about school.

After dinner, when they were alone, he said, "Now
why do you think you can't handle kids?"

"Are you forgetting bath time here?" she asked.

"Oh, yeah. Well, we seem to have that under control now."

"Of course we do, because Ariel's not in the tub and I'm not bathing her."

Ross shrugged and put his arm along the back of the sofa behind her. "Who cares who gives whom a bath?"

She smiled.

He saw the kids were occupied with their video and he leaned forward, saying, "Scratch that thought. I'd *love* to give you a bath."

She snorted with amusement.

He straightened. "Right. Bruise my ego."

"Impossible."

"Bruise anything you want, honey. I'd love it."

"You are a sick puppy."

Ariel's head came around. "A puppy! You have a puppy, 'Laine?"

"No, honey, I don't."

"I want a puppy," Ariel said in the saddest of voices.

"Oh, brother," Ross muttered.

"You do?" Elaine asked as the little girl came over and leaned on Elaine's legs.

"I do," Ariel said. "A brown puppy to love and love. Daddy says no. All the time Daddy says no."

"Because you don't take no for an answer," Ross retorted.

Ariel just smiled at Elaine. "I love a puppy."

"Hey, Dad," Jimmy said. "Why *can't* we have a puppy?"

"Oh, Lord," Ross muttered. "Not you, too."

Elaine looked at him, puzzled. "Is there some reason why they can't?"

"Yes," he replied. "We're barely home, which is very unfair to the dog. They need lots of training and attention."

"What about a cat?" she asked. "Cats are easy to take care of. Or so I've heard."

Ross groaned. "I'm allergic to cats."

"I don't want a cat," Ariel said.

"Me, neither," Jimmy added.

"Surely, some kind of pet would work," Elaine began.

"Okay, guys, time for bed," Ross commanded, hoping to stop the discussion before it got really out of hand.

He herded his children, protesting all the way, upstairs for the bath and bed routine. He also took the opportunity to talk with both of them about not utilizing a guest's presence as an opportunity to change his mind on closed subjects. He knew it was a lesson they'd never take to heart, no kid truly did, but it cooled their jets for a little while.

As soon as he returned to the living room, Elaine said, "I've done it again, haven't I? Contradicted you. I'm so sorry."

"You were an innocent led down the garden path by two experts." He kissed her tenderly. "Don't worry about it."

She sighed. "I can't help it."

"Then I must distract you." He kissed her again. And again. And again.

"I'm distracted," she murmured, with a deep sigh.

He tried to settle in with her and watch some television, but somehow the kissing got out of hand. Or rather, certain body parts got *in* his hands. His brain was sending some vague confusion about platonic relationships with Elaine, but the rest of him couldn't quite make out the signals.

Elaine wasn't helping him, either. She was so incredibly responsive to his touch that she sent his senses spinning. Before he knew it, her top had been shed and he was nuzzling her naked breasts. The rest of their clothes seemed to melt away. Prior promises to behave were lost in the current promise of delicious intimacy. Ross could no more resist Elaine than she could resist him.

He sat up and took her onto his lap, facing him. Her hair was tousled about her shoulders and her gaze dreamy. She smiled, then slowly absorbed into herself. Ross shuddered at the feel of her moist heat gripping him. He held her hips firmly and laved her breast with his tongue as they thrust together. It felt right, it was right for him to be with Elaine like this. She was all that mattered.

She arched against him, crying out as her passion spent itself out, her fingers clawing at his shoulders and hair. A dark wave washed through him, its hot liquid pushing him over the edge to join her. He breathed her name against her throat and held her tightly until wave after wave finally eased away.

It occurred to him, as he surfaced to reality and common sense, that his children might not be in their beds. He jerked his head to the stairs, then shuddered again.

"What?" Elaine murmured.

He chuckled and relaxed against her. "I was afraid the kids were down here."

She glanced up sharply. "Oh, God. I didn't even think of that. See how bad I am about kids?"

He grinned. "You're not bad. I'm just that good."

She nipped his neck, delightfully. "I wish I could

scoff at that, just to put your ego in its place, but I'd be lying.''

"I like an honest woman." He held her for a long moment, letting some old emotions run their course. He knew he was ready to take her to his bed. Besides, they'd better or dress and separate, an option he wasn't about to allow. "Before we have an audience, come upstairs.''

She smiled. "What's up there to stop it?''

"A lock on my bedroom door.''

She was off his lap in an instant and grabbing up clothes.

"Come on," she said. "What are you waiting for?''

"My legs to function for one thing," he replied. "Do you know how good you look naked? Bend over and pick up that bra.''

She flushed slightly. "Ross.''

"Okay.'' He got off the sofa and gathered up the rest. He sensed he didn't have quite her birthday-suit gracefulness.

They climbed the stairs, giggling together, mostly at Ross's wandering hands. They ran the gauntlet of the children's rooms without incident, Ross feeling his luck was with him. He shut his bedroom door behind them and smiled as Elaine turned to face him.

The future was in front of him. All he had to do was reach out and take it.

He did.

Chapter Nine

As Elaine woke, she was instantly aware of several things at the same time. The morning light was just coming through the curtains. Her bones were nonexistent in her body. A very warm, male form snuggled against her back. Something snored gently in her ear.

But she was most aware of a pair of wide, blue eyes staring at her from the side of the bed.

Panic shot through her as she looked back at Ariel, who casually leaned on the mattress edge and sucked her thumb. Elaine elbowed the man still wrapped in unconscious bliss.

Ross's snore cut off midway through its inhale stage. "What? What the—"

He stiffened, the words trailing away as he clearly caught sight of his daughter.

"Somebody forgot to lock the bedroom door," Elaine muttered, remembering how eager they'd been for each other.

"Ariel," Ross said, finding his voice again.

The child popped her thumb from her mouth. "Hi, Daddy. Did you think about the puppy?"

"Bribery," he muttered.

Elaine couldn't even laugh, too conscious of her nakedness under the sheet and geometric-patterned quilt. At least she woke up covered to the chin. She hated to think of the child's reaction if she hadn't been.

"Ariel," Ross went on. "What are you doing in here? Do you need something?"

"Just a puppy. Why is Elaine sleepin' here?"

"Ahhh…" Ross paused.

Elaine stepped in. "I wasn't feeling well and so we thought it would be better if I didn't drive home."

Ariel leaned over even more and reached out to play with Elaine's hair. "You could sleep in my bed."

"Thank you for the offer," Elaine said gravely, "I didn't want to make you sick."

Ariel nodded, clearly seeing the sense in that.

"Honey, why don't you go play in your room," Ross suggested.

"Daddy—"

"No argument, girl. Go play in your room."

"I'll be there in a little bit," Elaine promised.

Ariel grinned, obeying her father without further discussion.

When the bedroom door closed behind the child, Ross sighed with relief. "Oh, God. My worst nightmare."

Elaine rolled over to face him. "Hey. You didn't wake up with her staring at you."

"I couldn't handle it." He shuddered, then grinned at her. "I'd say 'good morning,' but I think we're beyond that."

"No kidding." She couldn't help smiling before she said, "I'm sorry, Ross. I truly meant to leave after…"

He kissed her gently. "It was too good to leave after that. I couldn't—"

The bedroom door opened again. This time Jimmy

entered the room. He eyed his father and Elaine, his expression unreadable.

"Ariel said Elaine was here," Jimmy announced. "I thought she was lying."

"Oh, no," Elaine murmured, heartsick at the overt awkwardness. Jimmy was only two years older than Ariel, but the nuances were different.

"Your sister, the informer, wasn't wrong, okay?" Ross said.

Jimmy grimaced. "I hate that."

"You hate what?" Ross asked, so matter-of-factly that Elaine didn't know what to think.

"Stupid Ariel." Jimmy turned, pulling the door behind him.

"That poor child," Elaine said. "Oh, God, Ross. I'm so sorry to put you and your family in this situation. Jimmy must be traumatized."

"I put them there, not just you," he replied. "I'm not so sure Jimmy's ready for a psychiatrist yet. He always calls his sister stupid when she's right about something. That bothers him more than you here."

"Oh." She slid from the bed, pulling the quilt with her and leaving him the sheet. She stood. "Ross, we...we shouldn't have done this, and not only because of the kids."

"Stop right there," he said, tossing back the sheet and getting out of bed.

His nakedness drew her hapless gaze. She wanted nothing more than for it to be last night again, the two of them intertwined in incredible lovemaking.

"I know we're supposed to be waiting until the bid is settled, but dammit, I'm sick of waiting," he told her. "It's a game you're no better at than I am, admit it."

She nodded. "Our feelings are too honest."

"Right. So let's give up this holding back. It's useless. We proved that last night. Three times."

She collapsed against the headboard in laughter. "It would have been four but I didn't have the heart to wake you."

"What?" he asked, reaching over and running his hands down her bare arms. "Don't tell me you went on without me."

"You'll never know."

"Damn, I'll never sleep again." He sobered. "You agree with me on this."

She sighed. "The genie's out of the bottle and too damn big to stuff back in. Yes. I do."

"Good." He hugged her.

"We can't flaunt it," she reminded him. "For your company's sake."

"I know."

"But the children—"

"Will accept a relationship between us." He straightened. "We'll be more careful around them, too."

She nodded.

"Well, now that we've solved the world's problems, let's have breakfast."

Elaine worried about the children's further reactions to her, but both seemed friendly. Ariel, especially, was still angling for a puppy, despite her father's cease-and-desist order. She wondered if she could help out there, so that Ariel could get her little heart's desire. The child was too precious to disappoint.

"I have to teach a class again tonight at my mother's store," he said, when she was finally leaving. "But how about dinner first? It'll be fast food with me and the kids.''

Elaine thought about all the meals her mother made that were piling up in her refrigerator. Healthy, low-fat meals that tasted delicious. ''I'd love to.''

''Good.''

When Elaine arrived home, she found a note from her mother.

> I see you've got extra meals left over from the last few weeks. I left you new ones this week. Why aren't you eating? You aren't doing that anorexia business, are you? You *must* eat nutritious meals.
>
> Love, Mom.

''I'm eating, I'm eating,'' Elaine muttered, flipping the note over her shoulder. Okay, so she was falling off the nutrition wagon tonight, but what the heck. A person had to fall off a wagon sometime.

She thought about her night with Ross. They had made love all night, seemingly endlessly until her body shivered with satisfaction at his simplest touch. Even with the shock of children alarm clocks, she had the underlying sense of rightness in waking up next to Ross. Everything with Ross had a rightness.

She was falling in love with him. Elaine knew it, didn't even try to deny it to herself. So many complications, so many reasons not to, so easy to get hurt again. This time she knew it would be the worst of all. She was older and wiser—supposed to be the latter, anyway. She had come into this relationship reluctantly, and she would pay dearly if it failed.

Elaine thrust the thought aside. She was also older

and wiser enough to at least enjoy what she had and not ask for more. So she would go to dinner with Ross and his family and she would wait for whatever came in the end.

That evening, after a meal overflowing in calories, salt and fat, Elaine thought her stomach would burst as they drove to Hardware and Muffins. If only her mother could see her now, she admitted ruefully, vowing never to indulge like a teenager again. Moderation in all things, although nothing was in moderation where Ross was concerned. Jimmy and Ariel looked normal, and she decided those cheery, kids meals must be less bloating and more nutritious. Next time she'd eat that. But mostly she had enjoyed her time with the three Steadwells.

"How often do you eat fast food?" she asked.

"Once every two weeks as a treat to the kids," he replied.

She smiled in relief. She could use a few antacid tablets right about now.

"Unless I'm pressed for time," he added. "Then it's whenever. Okay, so we're there at least once a week on average. Sometimes maybe two."

"You need to make meals and put them away," she said, thinking of the loaded freezer she had, courtesy of her mother.

He burst into laughter. "Elaine, honey, I'm lucky some days if I get in a shower, let alone cook a meal. I don't have the time to make up meals ahead. I wish I did."

"It could be another good topic for a Daddy Club lecture," she commented, not ready to let go of her theory. "And I have the perfect guest lecturer. My mother, Queen of the Freeze Aheads."

A voice erupted from the back seat, sending Ariel into spasms of delight. "My puppy says 'hello,' Daddy!"

"I heard him," Ross replied.

"Mine's name is Jimmy," Jimmy said.

"Mine's 'Laine," Ariel announced, not to be out-done by her brother.

Elaine smiled, very touched that Ariel had named the stuffed animal after her. She was also pleased that she had come up with the perfect solution to the puppy question. The fast-food place sold talking dachshunds, mostly promoting their chain. Elaine had bought one for each kid, giving them their "puppy." Ariel was ecstatic. Jimmy clearly liked his, which was enough for now.

Ross glanced over at her. "You're very smug, aren't you?"

"Yes, I am." She chuckled. "I think I made up for the ballet."

"Hey, far be it from me to eat crow but...Ariel still says something occasionally about the pretty fairy lady."

"What!" Elaine sat up, surprised.

Ross shrugged. "I guess she actually saw something between the bathroom trips. And Jimmy asked earlier today about going back to see the holiday lights."

"Yeah, can we?" he asked again from the back seat.

"Of course," Elaine said, turning around and not waiting for Ross to give permission. "Anytime you want."

"Tomorrow."

"You have school. We'll make a time," Ross assured him.

"We better," Jimmy threatened.

Elaine sat back in her seat, very pleased with herself. Maybe the jinx was wearing off her at last. Maybe she'd never be Superwife and Mom but she might just manage to not screw up too badly. Not enough to traumatize anyone.

Her common sense reminded her that she was getting way ahead of herself. She had no idea how Ross felt about her beyond an affection. They had that whole thing about business between them. And the kids had a say in the future as well.

At the store the present smacked them in the head with a two-by-four. They no sooner walked through the door than the kids raced ahead to show their grandmother their new "puppy."

Her grandmother had a visitor.

Burt Langdon looked from Elaine to Ross and back to Elaine again, his shrewd gaze taking in the cozy scene. Granted, she wasn't holding hands with Ross, let alone in his arms half-naked, but their relationship couldn't have been clearer.

"Elaine, you want to explain this," Burt said, grim faced. It didn't matter that he wore a casual leather coat, gray turtleneck sweater and heavy khakis, the man looked every inch the hard-nosed CEO he was.

"I'll explain," Ross began.

"It's not your business, Burt," Ruth Naomi said at the same time.

Burt chopped the air with one hand, then thrust a finger at Elaine. "You know the company policy. You explain. And don't hand me crap about being 'just friends.'"

Elaine's stomach churned. She knew her job was on the line. "I won't. I have a personal relationship with

Ross that started after we opened discussions with his company."

"Hot damn!" Ruth N. exclaimed, smiling happily.

"Grandma, you cursed," Jimmy reminded her. "We gotta play hardware helper. You promised."

"Mom, go take the kids and play hardware helper," Ross said.

"No flipping chance in—"

"Mom."

The word cracked like a whip. Burt's head jerked around to Ross, the man clearly taken aback by the authority exhibited.

Ruth N. eyed Ross for a moment. "Fine. Come on, kids. Margie wants to see your puppies."

"Yippee!" Ariel cheered, already running ahead.

"Is 'flipping' a curse?" Jimmy asked, as he and his grandmother walked away more sedately.

"Only the way I use it," Ruth N. replied.

When they were out of earshot, Elaine said, "I know what the company policy is, Burt. You don't have to cite it to me."

"Good." He looked at Ross. "I like you. I like what your company has to offer. But Data, Ink, has set up rules to avoid collusion between companies. We can't afford to be vulnerable. You understand?"

Ross thrust his jaw out, clearly not liking what Burt had to say. "Yes."

"Elaine, you'll see me in my office first thing tomorrow."

"If you're going to fire me, then fire me now," she told him, digging in her pride. She'd be damned before she'd spend a night worrying about her fate.

Burt made a face. "Hell, I'm not going to fire you. Not yet, anyway. Look, you two need to end this. I won't have any conflicts of interest. That's what I want to hear in the morning from you.'' He pointed his finger again, waving it between the two of them. ''End it. Tell Ruth Naomi I'll call her later.''

He stalked out of the store, taking his hurricane force with him.

Elaine slumped and put her hands over her eyes. ''Oh, God.''

''Bastard,'' Ross muttered, gazing out the glass front door.

''Cautious,'' Elaine countered, lifting her head and sighing. ''And I was having such a nice time.''

''I'm going with you tomorrow,'' Ross said. ''He's not going to get away with that.''

''Ross, he doesn't 'get away' with anything. He's the boss.'' She shook her head. ''Let's be honest here. I knew perfectly well there was a nonfraternization policy with the company. I understand why there's one. I don't want you to have any trouble about the contract. If there's any question about collusion, then the other companies bidding can cause a lot of legal hassles, especially someone who might figure out they'll never have the wherewithal to actually get awarded a Data, Ink, bid any other way.''

''I'm still going with you tomorrow,'' he said.

She shook her head. ''No. Absolutely not. Burt's a bear, but he respects people who stand on their own two feet with him. I learned that a long time ago. If you come in with me, he'll see me as weak and he *will* fire me.'' She smiled. ''I appreciate the White Knight gesture. I love it. But I need to be my own White Knight tomorrow.''

''I don't like it.''

She knew he was acquiescing, and she was glad.

Handling one cantankerous male was enough. "You call me right afterward, you understand."

She smiled. "I will. That's a promise."

He put his arm around her, and they stood silently together.

Finally she said, "Ross, we have to stop things now. For your sake. You won't get that bid if you don't. And I want you to have it. Dammit, I've been working hard for it."

"I hate this," he said.

She nodded. Her lip trembled. He ran his thumb, not his lips, across it to soothe away the pain, a gesture that already signaled acceptance of their doomed relationship.

"I'm giving your account to another manager, someone with no connection to you," she said.

Ross closed his eyes. "I can't go cold turkey on you."

She managed a watery chuckle. "We're going to have to."

Why did love cause so much pain?

"LOUSY WORKSHOP TONIGHT."

Ross growled at his mother's assessment of his teaching skills. "I told you I didn't want to do a thing on pipe sweating. My plumbing skills suck."

"No wonder Elaine broke it off with you."

"Ha-ha. Wonderful double entendre, Mother. Next time get a life."

He slammed a piece of pipe into the odds-and-ends box they used for demonstration purposes.

"Honey, don't shoot the messenger," Ruth Naomi said.

Ross gritted his teeth together. He wanted to shoot

somebody. Elaine had called him after soothing Burt's ruffled policy feathers. His company's proposal was in no jeopardy, and she still had her job. Someone named Todd was handling RP Computers now. Ross had spoken with him; he seemed to be a nice guy and eager about Ross's company. But the whole arrangement stunk. It disgusted him that in this day and age of personal enlightenment, someone else could dictate his private life. His own acceptance of that disgusted him more. He should have been the one in Burt's office. He should have called the whole deal off and kept Elaine. Granted they would need *two* jobs, but he could have lived with himself afterward. Instead, he'd done nothing.

Two weeks had gone by and he hadn't seen or heard from her. Neither had he called or sought her out. Thanksgiving had passed without an acknowledgment from either of them. He felt like a wimp, a betrayer, a bastard of the first water, hooked on money to the point of losing his moral compass.

"You know what your problem is?"

His mother's question was clearly rhetorical, but Ross answered, anyway. "I'm not a singer in a rock and roll band?"

"Nope, although it'd be interesting to see you be Peter Pan for once. Nope, your problem is Elaine. Or lack of Elaine."

"Could we get off this topic? My intimate life is the last thing I want to talk about with my mother."

His mother grinned, unrepentant. "Nobody likes to think their children or their parents are having sex. I always thought I was a virgin birth.

Can you imagine your grandparents doing the naked hula?"

"Oh, God, Mom." He started laughing, not able to help himself, at the thought of his sweet elderly grandparents in the throes of primal urges. "You're right. You had to be a virgin birth."

"Nope. They were doing the wild thing right up until the end. In fact that was your grandfather's end. He had a massive heart attack during sex. He came and he went."

"You're kidding!"

Ruth N. shook her head. "I wish. No, your grandmother told me herself before the funeral. Believe me, that was more information than I ever needed to know about my parents."

Ross put another pipe in the box, this time with less force. He felt a little better, a very little better, at his mother's story.

"I wasn't talking about your sex life, anyway, although when you opened the door I couldn't resist running with it," she said. "I meant that you're in love with Elaine."

Ross straightened and looked at his mother. Her expression brooked no nonsense. She was serious.

"Mom..." he began, wanting to say something yet feeling overwhelmed by the notion.

"You're passionately in love with her. Anyone can see you are." She patted him on the shoulder. "Give yourself a little time to think about it. You'll know I'm right. Here, give me that."

She took the box from him and carried it into the back room. Ross stood in the middle of the workshop area and watched her go. His mind was doing exactly as she ordered.

Could he be in love with Elaine?

He loved the way she walked into a room. He adored

the way she handled herself, strong and sure. He worshiped her ability to adjust to any situation. He couldn't wait to talk with her every day. He even loved being exasperated with her. He wanted her deeply, passionately, every waking minute.

He pondered the notion his mother had put in his head over the next few days. While the positive points exerted themselves instantly, the negatives slowly crept in.

When he took the kids to the latest computer-animated phenomenon of a movie, he was reminded of her choice of children's entertainment. While Ariel could talk about the "pretty fairy" and Jimmy could ask to see the holiday lights, that night of endless whining and bathroom runs was still vivid in his mind. Elaine had spoken a lot about her inability to relate to children, but she had tried so hard to make that night work. Unfortunately it hadn't, confirming her own opinion of herself.

Cooking a simple dinner also brought home the fact that Elaine's mother made all her meals for her. Even with a lesson or two, she still had a long way to go to make spaghetti and meatballs.

Two former marriages, no matter how well he understood their demise, showed further still a lack of domestic judgment.

But the biggest question of all was his own excess baggage. Was he ready to be in love again? Was he ready to accept that anything could happen to her at any moment and he would be bereft? Ross's whole mind recoiled from the knowledge that life had no guarantees where love was concerned. It hurt worse this second time, to even think of losing a mate again, because he *knew* what he would go through. And could he put the kids through it a second time? Losing their mother had been helped a little because they had been so young when she died. Their memories were vague about her. But to give them a mother now, then lose her…Ariel would be devastated this time. Jimmy even more so because he was less bewildered than his sister had been.

"Didcha see that birdie talk, Daddy?" Ariel asked, as they left the movie.

"Oh, ah, yes." The movie was more a great place to think than to watch.

"He was just being silly," Ariel added.

"You're just being silly," Ross told her. This their new routine together. He took her hand.

"No, *you're* just being silly." Ariel giggled.

"You're both being silly," Jimmy said. "Hey, Dad, can we go to the mall?"

"Sure." What the heck, he thought. It was Saturday afternoon and he only had laundry waiting at home. Piles of it. Tonight, since he wasn't busy, he would take care of clothes washing. "You want me to buy you something there?"

Jimmy had the grace to look guilty. "I was thinking about it."

"Buy for me, Daddy!" Ariel demanded.

"Spoiled, my chick." He tweaked her cheek. "That's what you are."

Ariel skipped happily to the car, nonplussed at his assessment.

The mall was crowded, the holiday shopping having started in earnest. Ross held Ariel's hand firmly, yet let her pull him where she wanted to go. He knew if he didn't, she'd manage to break away to look at something and she'd be gone in a flash. He warned Jimmy to stay close and reminded the boy early and often if he looked ready to race ahead.

"What's that?" Ariel asked, pointing to a playhouse in the middle of a courtyard area. It was decorated in candy canes and gingerbread men. A long line of children and parents wound back nearly to the far store fronts.

"Santa, you dummy," Jimmy scoffed at his little sister. "Dad, can we go see Santa? Please, please, please!"

Jimmy raced off to the end of the line without waiting for an answer.

As he and Ariel walked over to join Jimmy, Ross looked with dismay at the kids before his son. "Jimmy, that's a big crowd in front of us. You're going to have a long wait. How about we come back first thing tomorrow morning to see Santa?"

Jimmy shook his head, his chin up, his gaze steady on the prize: the doorway to magic. His feet were solidly planted on the shining tiles, his stance as stiff as any Marine's. "I can wait, Dad."

Ross had a feeling the boy could. The damper, however, was holding hands with him. "Jimmy, there's another problem. Ariel. She's pretty little to wait a long time—"

"I'll wait, Dad." The high, piping voice was a dead-on imitation of her brother's. So was Ariel's stance. Her gaze, however, was wide-eyed.

Ross realized it was her first true Christmas, the one where she was of an age to appreciate all aspects of it—and remember long afterward. He decided, against better judgment, to let things ride.

The line moved slowly, very slowly. Jimmy went over his list five times with Ross, every toy wanted in detail so there would be no mistake. Ariel, realizing she'd actually have to speak to the big guy, started making a list. Fortunately, at three, it was a short one.

"Daddy, I'm tired," Ariel said finally, giving the signal Ross had been dreading.

Jimmy rounded on her. "We ain't leavin'!"

Ariel backed up, startled by her brother's command.

"Here, honey, I'll hold you," Ross offered, bending down to pick her up.

Ariel's chin firmed mulishly. "No."

He had a couple of tough guys.

"Hi."

Ross turned, but he didn't need to see Elaine standing behind him, to have a deep shock of pleasure run through him. Her voice did it all on its own. Shopping bags hung from her hands.

"'Laine!"

Ariel flung her arms around Elaine's legs. Fortunately, Elaine also had the Marine's stance down pat now, and she didn't budge from her spot. She patted the child on the back, a bright blue bag banging lightly against Ariel's back.

"Hi. You going to see Santa?"

"Oh, yes," Ariel said happily. "I'm gonna tell him what I want for Christmas."

She proceeded to tell Elaine all the things she wanted, clearly having them down pat.

"I'm telling Santa first," Jimmy announced. He grinned at Elaine, a·clear greeting but one that didn't detract from his goal.

Ariel stuck her tongue out at her brother, who told Elaine his list, a longer one but not unreasonable.

"Wow," Elaine said. "It sounds like a plan."

"Yup," Jimmy said with satisfaction.

"Yup," Ariel repeated, truly having no clue.

"How are you?" Ross asked, his voice low.

"Okay." She sighed, belying the positive word. "How's it going with Todd? Are you getting along all right with him? Is he making sure to push the proposal along?"

"He's good," Ross said. "You were better."

She flushed slightly, but smiled. "Thanks."

"I've missed you."

Ross didn't try to hide his hunger for her. His mother's words flashed in his brain. Love. Looking at Elaine, he wondered what the hell scared him about it. And if it really mattered.

Elaine grimaced. "I know. I hate this."

"I suppose this is collusion."

"To hell with them."

Ross laughed. "Well, you can keep me company while the kids see Santa. Can't you?"

"Sure. Besides, I don't think Ariel's letting me go." The child still had one arm wrapped around Elaine's jeans. Ariel's thumb was in her mouth, content.

Ross smiled and ruffled Jimmy's hair. He reached for Elaine's bags. "Here. Let me take them."

Their fingers touched as the packages shifted from her hands to his. The sudden sizzle of skin to skin, however innocent, knocked Ross's senses out of balance. He was never ready for it, and he hoped he never would be. She looked at him, the same shock of recognition in her eyes that he knew must be in his. One touch and she could send him spinning for life.

They didn't talk much between them, Ross not needing words. He only needed her presence to feel complete. The kids chatted with her, easily, which gave him great pleasure to watch. All the cautions didn't mean anything at the moment.

The kids finally got to the front of the line, Elaine's presence getting them all past the frustration stage. The woman at the door was dressed in a green-and-red outfit of the most sumptuous material Ross had ever seen. The cloth had a sparkle that seemed otherworldly. Even her elfen ear points looked so real that Ross couldn't see where the flesh left off and the prosthesis began.

"I'm Holly," the elf said, grinning widely as if she thrived on whining children and exasperated adults. "Now, let me see…"

She took Jimmy's and Ariel's chins and lifted their faces up, examining them thoroughly. Ross had the oddest feeling that she was seeing into their hearts. Holly the elf smiled and caressed their cheeks.

"My, my, such big wishes." She leaned down and added, "You will have your heart's content. I promise, and an elf never lies."

Ross frowned at the woman, concerned that she would stir the kids up into asking for something impossible. Right now he could manage what they wanted.

"I just love this time of year," she said to Ross and Elaine. "Old Nick gives me the magic back for a little bit."

"Better you than me," Elaine said, shivering as a child screamed farther back in the long line.

Holly looked at her. "Too late. You're already hooked, and you'll be just fine."

She looked at Ross, then smiled. "Yours is coming."

Ross stared at her. He hoped she was right.

Chapter Ten

What an odd thing for the elf woman to say.

And right on the money, Elaine thought. She felt as if she was drowning in misery. It was too late for her. She was in love with Ross.

As she trudged along in the aftermath of the Santa visit, she felt her whole world was collapsing. Maybe it was brought home to her because Ariel held her hand tightly as they walked together, and the child chattered about seeing Santa. Maybe it was the way Jimmy tried to wheedle toys and games out of his father. The boy was very funny and endearing, as well as exasperating for Ross.

Maybe it was the way Ross took every opportunity to touch her. He brushed her hair back from her cheek. He rubbed her arm occasionally. He put his hand on the small of her back to guide her through the crowd. Each touch sent her senses spiraling. Each touch reminded her of how forbidden it was—for the moment.

Leave it to Burt, she thought, to set man-woman relationships back to the Middle Ages. He *would* pull Ross's bid because of a personal connection. Elaine just couldn't have that on her conscience. And so here they were, longing to be with each other and yet having to restrain their feelings.

"Don't think about it," Ross whispered in her ear.

"How could you tell?" she asked, smiling sadly.

"Just by the expression on your face."

"I shouldn't even be here like this."

"We're not doing anything but walking around the mall." He pushed her hair back once again from her cheek, just a touch to touch.

"I know. But it's dangerous because Burt could misinterpret us together like this if he found out. And... being with you could lead to things."

He didn't deny it. "Look at the big stuffed bear in the toy store window."

She looked at the bear, wondering why he suggested it. Her hair was swept back, and lips pressed against the nape of her neck. Hot breath caressed her skin, sending her restraint spinning into dust. As she saw their reflection, so tender and so sensuous, Elaine's knees weakened and she thought she would collapse.

"Dad!" Jimmy wailed, catching sight of his father kissing Elaine.

Ross straightened. "And here I was just thinking you need a new micro car."

"I was thinkin' the same thing," Jimmy agreed, clamming up against any protest he was about to make about what he had just seen. He smiled brilliantly at Elaine, looking quite content to have his father kissing her.

"Isn't that bribery?" Elaine asked Ross.

Ross shrugged. "Sometimes it's called good parenting."

"When?"

"Well, that's the trick. Now look at the bear again." He leaned over and kissed her fully on the lips.

"I love that bear," she said, sighing.

"Me, too," Ariel said. "Okay, Daddy, kiss me."

"She's learning." He bent down and gave her a huge buss on the lips. "I love you."

"I wuv you, too," Ariel said.

Ross stood. He stared at Elaine. Suddenly she knew he was sending a message of love to her. She knew it as she knew herself.

"Oh, God," she said out loud at the timing of it. They couldn't admit to love right now, not when they had to be platonic acquaintances. "You can't... We can't... I do, too."

Ross's expression changed, like the proverbial light-bulb going off in his head. Her own message had been received. "Oh, God."

"We're in trouble now." How were they supposed to stay apart after that realization? But she began to smile, all the difficulties fading into the background at the thought that he loved her. Her, the domestic un-goddess. He loved her.

"Real trouble. Come back to the house with us. We need to talk."

"We won't talk and you know it," she said, caution welling up inside her.

"And your point would be?" he asked, grinning like a wolf about to eat his dinner.

God, but she hoped so, feeling like a happy sacrificial lamb.

"Dad, the car!" Jimmy prompted, clearly having had enough of talk he didn't understand.

"Right, the car."

They left the mall shortly afterward. As common

sense returned, Elaine managed to drive to her house rather than his that evening. They really did have to be careful until the bid was settled. But when she walked through her front door, the silence deafened her. She sat down in a living room chair and listened to nothing. Nothing had been her private life for far too long.

Now somebody loved her. She examined it from all the angles, trying to find the impulse, the chink that said the love was based on something other than her. She couldn't find it. In truth, she and Ross were opposites in so many ways that they shouldn't be in love with each other.

Her telephone rang, and she snatched it up.

"Okay," he said. "Okay, you went home instead of coming here. I thought something happened to you."

"No." She gave a watery chuckle, the emotions overcoming her for a moment. "I wanted to, but I didn't for your sake. It was terrible not to be able to touch you when we realized how we felt about each other. I knew we wouldn't be able to stop things if I went to your house."

He had harsh words about "his sake," ending with, "Damn Burt. This is ridiculous. I love you, but I can't be with you because of some antiquated fraternization rules."

She grinned and settled back in the chair, the town house seemingly filled with happy noise. "I love you, too. When did this happen?"

"Hell, I don't know." He laughed. "Listen to us. We sound like a couple of nuts."

"No, just a couple of business realists, because I won't let you lose this bid."

"I don't give a damn about that. I won't let you lose your job."

"Impasse. That's why I'm here and you're there."

"But I want you here. With me. Saying I love you."

Oh, God, she thought. "How am I supposed to fight that?"

"You're not." His whisky voice worked its magic. "Elaine, why can't we be together one time? I need to *know* you feel the same way I do."

"I just want to be with you," she said.

"Only for tonight. Then we'll be good."

He could be *very* good. And she couldn't stand the aloneness of her house a minute longer. One time couldn't hurt. After all, Burt didn't have a twenty-four-hour watch on them.

How she didn't get a ticket for reckless driving, Elaine never knew. She only knew she could no more stand being apart from Ross than he from her. He had the front door already open, the cold December air blowing into the house. He stood in the frame, his silhouette outlined by the light shining behind him. He looked virile and beautiful. Elaine went into his arms without hesitation. He kissed her, their tongues rubbing gently against each other in an intimate promise.

When he lifted his head, he said, "You love me."

"God, yes," she murmured, smiling. "And you love me, a two-time domestic loser."

He chuckled. "You're in the winner's circle now, kid."

"What a mess," she said, as he rubbed her back. They still stood in the doorway, unaffected by the cold.

"We'll work on it," he replied.

She laughed. It felt so right to be in his embrace that she wasn't going to worry about all the things plaguing their relationship. Either they worked out—or they didn't.

"We'll have to be discreet," she reminded him.
"For your sake."

"And yours."

She raised her head. "Love me now."

He pushed the door shut and closed them off from
the world.

THREE MORNINGS LATER, Elaine was still happily hum-
ming to herself as she walked down the corridor of
Data, Ink's purchasing section. Her body and mind
hadn't come down to earth yet, from the revelation and
the aftermath. She'd had no clue how much sweeter
the lovemaking was when true love was involved. It
held an innocence that took a person's breath away.
Her assistant, Tina, said she looked as if she was float-
ing on air. But she couldn't hide her emotions. She
didn't want to.

"Elaine!"

Burt's bark held all the bite it needed to send her
into a tailspin. She whipped around to find him coming
out of one of the offices, his sharp gaze piercing her
secrets.

"Your office. Now."

He strode off down the corridor, not waiting for her
to even acknowledge him. He didn't have to. Heads
popped up from the cubicles, everyone looking to see
what was happening.

Elaine's heart fluttered. She felt as if she'd been
kicked in the solar plexus and wanted nothing more
than to be sick in the ladies' room.

He couldn't know, she thought. They had been extremely discreet. She hadn't even gone to the hardware
store, not even for a Hardware for Women Koffee
Klatch seminar on installing a light switch. She had

two that didn't work. He was just bellowing to bellow. Burt handled everything at the same decibel level.

She lifted her chin and walked after him, although he had long disappeared down the corridor. When she reached her outer office, Tina looked shaken, the girl's mouth pulled wide in a grimace of dismay. She simply pointed to Elaine's private office.

"He slammed the door," Tina whispered.

"I hope he got hit for big-time alimony," Elaine whispered back. She'd much rather her boss be upset over his private life and need a friend, rather than *she* be in big trouble for something.

Elaine took a deep breath, straightened her jacket, smoothed her skirt, delayed as long as she could, then screwed up her courage in a tight knot and strode into her office.

Burt sat in her chair, leaning back in a casual position, clearly signaling to whom she owed that chair...and her job. It was a classic power play. Elaine eyed him, forcing herself to stay calm.

"I hope that's comfortable for you," she said, "although I keep it much lower to the ground than your chair is, I'm sure."

Burt's jaw thrust out in irritation before he said, "I saw Ruth Naomi last night."

Elaine started to relax. Ross's mother no doubt frustrated him.

"You didn't dissolve that relationship."

Elaine stilled.

"I see you don't deny it. What the hell did you think you were doing?" His voice rose. "This company was founded on honesty! We don't even take five-dollar gifts from other companies in a bid for our services. And you're out there, sleeping with that guy—"

"That's enough," Elaine snapped, not wanting him to turn something right into something tawdry.

"That's not enough! I told you to stop it. You haven't. His bid's out."

"No, it isn't," Elaine countered, although her insides crawled with fear for Ross. "I will excuse myself from the bid selection process. Ross's bid now has nothing to do with me."

"That doesn't cut it."

"You want me to be the whipping girl here and get fired?" she asked. "Okay. But I will have a job with your rival in a heartbeat."

"You signed a noncompetition clause—"

"I don't need to divulge anything from here, Burt, to make another company successful. I only have to work as hard for them as I've worked for you." She waved a hand. "You'll never get anyone to run this department as efficiently as I have. Wasn't that what you said in my last personnel eval? I'll rachet up to speed with a new company in no time, and it won't be with a company who has antiquated rules of behavior. You can't put people together and not expect interaction, Burt. Even you have violated your own policies in this."

Her chair flipped upright. "Me!"

"You're doing your best to fraternize with his mother. That's collusion if I ever saw it. It's worse, because Ross has no control over that, and yet you can dump out his bid like water from a faucet. If you're worried about lawsuits, I think he had the perfect one. *You* went after his mother; she didn't seek you out. You need to fire yourself for policy violation before you dismiss his bid. Or cut yourself off from Ruth Naomi. Are you ready to do that?"

Burt looked at her, his mouth in a grim line.

"Burt, people come together," she said more softly. "They can't help how they feel. We have people here who have relationships with people from other companies. They find someone and they care about them. What is wrong with that? Nothing. There're lots of ways to avoid a charge of collusion from a losing bidder in this situation."

"How?" he asked.

She was scrambling and she knew it. But he was listening and that was more important. "I think we should both excuse ourselves from the bidding selection process. Appoint someone who has no connection with RP Computers or Ross or Ruth Naomi to oversee the bid process. Better still, let it be selection by a committee that will have to work with the product after we buy it. They're the ones who really know what they need. We could make criteria that bidders must meet in order to have consideration. Make it tough. That you or I or anyone has contact shouldn't matter then because if the criteria aren't completely checked off, they're out. It should eliminate any business advantage to a personal relationship."

"Came up with that off the top of your head, didn't you?"

She grinned. "I work well under pressure."

"That's why I like you." He grinned ruefully and shook his head. "Damn, but I think you might have gotten hold of something here."

"I try."

He wasn't through with her yet. "I didn't appreciate the threat about what you'd do with another company."

"It wasn't a threat, Burt. It was a promise. Why wouldn't I work hard for them?"

Burt chuckled. "That's what worried me. Wait! Who comes up with the criteria?"

"Me and you. The committee finalizes them."

"Mmm. Who appoints the committee?"

She thought about that one. "No one. All the managers are automatically on the committee, with the section manager most affected by the bid having two votes in the selection. And you would have two votes as well, just to ensure a balance."

"As CEO, I ought to, anyway." He mulled her plan over. "One thing, this way means the lowest bid isn't necessarily the winner."

"Burt, sometimes the lowest bid costs more in the long run."

"So we're finding out."

She refrained from saying "I told you so." She'd expressed reservations about the Dall Computers bid last year. Instead she said, "Can I have my chair back now?"

He eyed her but didn't move. "Is it the real thing with this guy?"

"I don't know," Elaine replied, wanting to be very honest. "We've got a lot of other things to sort out eventually."

Things that scared her.

"You're going to bat for a guy who may not be worth it."

Elaine smiled. "He's worth it. That's the part I'm sure of."

"I DIDN'T MEAN TO."

Ruth Naomi's stricken face was all Ross needed to see to know his mother *had* had a major slip of the tongue with Burt.

"He was here," Ruth N. added, rushing in with an explanation that would no doubt absolve her from wrongdoing. In her mind at least. "He's been here a lot, underfoot. We were just talking, about his kids mostly. And I mentioned the cute story you told me about the kids going to see Santa. As soon as I said Elaine's name, I tried to backtrack on it, but he was quick. Boy, he's got a temper."

Fortunately, Burt Langdon had a reasoning brain, Ross acknowledged. Elaine had called him and told him about the conversation she'd had with her boss. He'd dumped everything and rushed over to Hardware and Muffins to get at the bottom of it. He knew he had to see his mother face-to-face to find out how much damage she'd done. Now, sitting across from her at a table by the coffee bar, he had all his fears realized.

"You look just like your father," Ruth Naomi said. "Whenever I was in trouble with him."

"You're lucky, Mom." He ran his fingers through his hair. "Hell, I'm lucky not to have lost the bid. Elaine's lucky not to have lost her job."

"Well, that's ridiculous." His mother looked outraged. "Over a private relationship? I'd have been in his office with a whip and a chain to beat some sense into him."

"Subtle, Mom. Very subtle." He thought about what else Elaine had told him and he scowled.

"Okay. Where else did I screw up?"

"Not you, Mom." He shrugged. "Actually, it's not a bad thing that came out of this, but Data, Ink, will now have criteria every bidding company has to make. They also will have a committee that makes the decision on the bids. It levels the playing field."

"Then it's not a bad thing," his mother said.

"It could knock RP Computers right out of the job."
His mother cursed heartily.

"Good thing the kids aren't here or you'd be corrupting them again."

"As long as I'm consistent." His mother frowned, clearly worried. "I pray I didn't do anything that would keep you from getting this job. I know how hard you're working on it. Do you want me to talk to Burt?"

"Hell, no, Mom." He truly only wanted to impress upon her the need for caution, not panic. "It's okay, ultimately. The best thing is Elaine and I no longer have to hide away. Not that we could have."

"No, you couldn't." She propped her elbow on the table and her hand on her cheek. "What do I do with Burt, though? He's a nice man, but a lonely one on the rebound. That's not for me."

Thank God for cast-iron criteria, Ross thought. He could easily envision his mother's reluctance with Burt as a second bid jeopardy. Maybe the greatest one. "Have you told him this?"

"Hell, yes." She pursed her lips. "He says he understands but he keeps coming around, asking me out for coffee."

"Maybe he only wants coffee."

"Don't bet on it. The man's horny."

"Mom, please." Ross shuddered, just not able to see his mother as the object of a strong sexual attraction for a man. He much preferred to leave that to Oedipus.

His mother straightened. Ross could almost hear a cartoon lightbulb going off above her head. "It doesn't matter now, right? I can just tell him to buzz off, and you won't have to pay for it. I was trying to be diplomatic."

The notion of his mother being diplomatic gave Ross

the willies even more. "Damn, Mom, you could really screw this up."

"Hey, I've been a diplomat plenty of times."

"For who? The Balkans?" He decided to get deadly serious. "Mom, if you're going to let him down, just do it real, real easy. *Real* easy."

The fear was still in his head when he picked up Elaine for their first official date. No business. No kids. His mother was baby-sitting. And no hiding out.

"How does Burt feel about my mother?" he asked her, when they settled in their seats for a movie. The house lights were half-lit, the screen flashing questions and local advertisements, to keep moviegoers entertained while they waited.

"He's got a crush." She sounded amused.

"It's not reciprocal and she's been telling him that. You don't think I'll have another set of criteria to meet?"

"No. I'll make sure you don't."

"I can't believe you went in there by yourself and handled him."

She eyed him. "Ross, I'm not helpless."

"I know that. I feel bad that I wasn't with you." He grinned ruefully. "But your criteria are killing us."

Elaine grinned back. "You'll live with them, if you want the job."

"I'll live with them because I love you."

She leaned over and kissed him. "I love you, too. Hang in there. This will be just as tough for Dall Computers to meet. Maybe tougher."

Ross chuckled happily. One of the criteria Data, Ink, required was a discount for computers not yet shipped, if the market price of the hardware dropped anytime over the life of the contract. Maybe they would beat the corporate monster yet.

"Ross, do you think it means anything that we're doing this relationship backward?" she asked as they settled in for a movie. "Other than we've made a royal mess of things."

"Na." He put his arm around her and pulled her close. As close as he could with an armrest between them. "When I was a kid, my arm nearly fell off the first time I took a girl to a movie. How R rated is this movie? Sex or violence?"

"Both," she replied. "It's a Bruce Willis film."

"Good." He grinned, his arm already giving the first stirring of a protest. "So how did you like your first official-date dinner?"

"Venus and the Cowboy was terrific," Elaine said, mentioning the new, hot Philadelphia eatery. "When the chef was at The Striped Bass we saw her there. Burt was on a fish kick for a while."

"No Burt talk."

"Right."

The theater went dark and the first movie trailers began. Ross stole some popcorn from Elaine's minibag. She took his hand and licked his fingers, one by one, her tongue curling moistly around his flesh. Sweat popped out on his forehead.

"I love butter," she finally murmured.

"I'll smear myself in it when we get home."

"Yum. What's your favorite thing to eat at the movies?"

He laughed. "Skittles."

"But you didn't get any tonight."

"I'm full from dinner. Full from you."

She smiled. "You just want sex."

"Damn straight."

"I don't do sex on the first date."

"Then it's a good thing we had sex before we had a date."

She pressed her face into his shoulder, shaking with laughter. Finally she lifted her head. "You're a wicked man."

And he proved it during the movie. At one point, Ross slowly slid his hand up her leg, cursing the jeans that kept him ever so slightly distant from her satiny skin.

"We're too old for this," she whispered in his ear.

He grinned. "No, you're not."

"But someone will see. People walk up and down...oh, my...the aisles."

"Good thing it's dark in here then."

They touched and petted like teenagers, not doing a very good job of hiding their feelings for each other. Ross loved this newfound playfulness and felt as though the past years had been shed at last from his shoulders. Nothing, he thought, would take Elaine away from him.

Driving to her house seemed an eternity. He couldn't wait any longer for her.

She no sooner unlocked her front door, than he whisked her inside, pushing the door shut behind them. He kissed her frantically, all the fooling around finally culminating into a desperate need. His hands worked her jeans snap and zipper until his fingers were underneath her panties to her silky woman's flesh. She pushed his shirt up, her palms finding his nipples and rubbing them lightly. Sensations pulsed through him.

Somehow they made it upstairs to her bedroom.

Somehow they got all their clothes off. He sank into her warmth and knew he could not stop himself.

"Sorry, sorry," he murmured, apologizing for the need that couldn't wait for the niceties.

"Now!" she demanded back, already thrusting against him.

He thrust into her, harder and harder, faster and faster, his body driving him in a frenzy of movement. Elaine clung to him, whispering her need and love. When he stiffened and moaned, his body pulsating as it released itself into hers, she held him tightly, murmuring her own pleasure.

Exhausted, he slumped against the door, his legs like water as his body calmed down.

"I love you," she whispered. "I love saying it to you."

He smiled to himself. "I couldn't ask for more."

He really couldn't. Everything was bound to work out.

Chapter Eleven

"Stop bringing them toys."

Ross's exasperation was clear—and serious. Elaine had just given a couple of "overheard" Santa requests to Jimmy and Ariel. She knew he meant she was trying to ease her way into their life, but that wasn't true. She just liked giving them things and seeing their faces light up with pleasure.

"I'm sorry," she said. "I had no idea how much fun it was to give kids things."

"You're trying to buy their love."

"No." She shook her head, going into the kitchen to get their dinner ready. They had been trading off dinners for several weeks, and the meal was at her house tonight. "Maybe I want help with their acceptance of me, but I'm not buying love."

"You only have to be yourself," he said, following her into the kitchen. He paused, spotting something. "Don't tell me you got your mother to make dinner again for us."

"Who? Me?" She ignored the four plastic containers defrosting on her counter. "Never."

It was no lie. She had taken out meals her mother had made for the week for her, not for his family.

He picked one up. "What's this? Turkey tetrazzini? Who's having that? Ariel?"

"Well, that meat loaf I cooked wasn't great," she replied.

"It was fine," he said.

She smiled, pleased that he thought her cooking skills were coming along. "I had to stay late again, so I went this route. This is better, anyway, believe me, because my mother made it. Even Ariel will like the turkey more than anything I make."

"Your mom probably hates me for all the extra work," Ross said.

No, Elaine thought ruefully. Her mother liked Ross. It was Elaine's lack of ability she didn't like. Instead, she took every opportunity to point out her daughter's domestic shortcomings and refused to see any progress in her daughter. The maternal Greek chorus constantly asked, "What are you going to do when you have to cook every night? What are you going to do when you have to buy clothes for children? What are you going to do when they have no clean clothes? What are you going to do when the children fight? What are you going to do when they get bad grades in school? Or they hang out with a bad crowd?"

The list of domestic responsibilities was endless. Elaine would think she was making progress in one area, then her mother would come along and point out seven others Elaine hadn't even thought of. She was new at all this, her confidence shaky at best, and her mother's litany scared her. While Elaine was the solution think tank at the office, at home she felt like the dumb bunny.

"My mom likes you, Ross," Elaine said finally.

"You had to think about it."

She laughed wryly. "I had to think about how much she's not happy with me."

"Why?"

Jimmy came racing into the room. "What's for dinner?"

"Well, son, you have a choice," Ross replied. He held up a container. "Turkey tetrazzini."

"Bleck!"

Ross displayed another one. "Chicken *cordon bleu.*"

"Blue chicken!" Jimmy scoffed. "No way."

Ross read off another marked container. "Orange Dover sole."

"I'm not eatin' an orange shoe!" Jimmy exclaimed.

"And finally…" Ross squinted at the label. "Pork surprise."

"Double bleck!"

"I think I'll pass, too."

"It's very good," Elaine protested, dismayed that dinner wouldn't be the success she'd hoped. Or at least the neutral meal she needed. She sighed. "I'll call the pizza place."

"We had pizza last night," Ross said.

"Okay. Burgers."

"I'm tired of them," Jimmy told her.

"Okay. Chinese."

"I hate that stuff," Jimmy announced, squelching the idea before it started.

"Ariel's not crazy about it, either," Ross added, putting the nail in the Chinese coffin.

"I don't know what to do," Elaine said, starting to panic.

Ross shrugged. "We'll eat anything."

"Ross!"

"Almost. Hell, okay. I'll take the pork thing. Jimmy, the chicken has bread and ham and cheese inside it, nothing strange and nothing you don't like. You can eat it."

"No, way."

"Yes, way."

"Ariel..." He looked between the two remaining containers. "Got any peanut butter and jelly?"

"I want that," Jimmy said.

Elaine gave up. This was another fine mess she'd gotten herself into. "I have peanut butter but no jelly. Just orange marmalade."

Jimmy made a rude noise, clearly giving his thumbs-down on the marmalade.

"Hey," Elaine said. "I like it."

"You're weird."

Jimmy's opinion held no humor to it, no light family fun. Elaine felt it stab her heart.

"Name-calling is unacceptable, son," Ross said.

Jimmy just looked at his father.

"Jimmy."

Jimmy turned to Elaine, thrusting his jaw out mul-ishly for a moment.

"I'm sorry I said you were weird. Your food's weird. Dad, I'm not saying I'm sorry for the truth. You said I never should."

Ross looked heavenward, clearly dismayed at having his words come home to roost with him. Elaine sighed with resignation.

"Jimmy, I'm not offended that you think my food's weird. I guess I would think that, if I were five again. Matter of fact, I hated pork surprise when I was your age, but my mother made me eat it and I liked it...eventually. Okay, at least dinner's solved. For to-

night. Tomorrow, we're at your house so we'll eat better.''

"You'll get another cooking lesson," Ross promised, smiling at her.

"Tomorrow my class goes to the touching place,"
Jimmy announced, obviously ready to chat now that
the menu was solved.

"A touching place?" Elaine asking, worried about
a thing with that sort of name.

"The Please Touch Museum," Ross replied, clari-
fying beautifully. "In Philly. Damn! My mother told
me she couldn't pick him up from school tomorrow
because she's going on a special bus trip to New York
to see a play, but I forgot and scheduled an important
meeting for tomorrow afternoon. I can't get out of it.''

"Trying to hook up with my competitors?" Elaine
asked, teasing him.

Ross grinned and stroked her fingers, sending shivers
of sensual delight through her system. "Absolutely.
Hey, we'll sell to anybody." He looked at her, his expression serious. His face was so intense and so hand-
some that Elaine felt her heart speed up with anticipation. He then said, "Honey, could you get Jimmy
from school tomorrow and take him to the store? My
mother might not be there, but Marge is running the
place and she's watching him and Ariel. She just can't
leave and pick him up. I hate to ask, but I'm in a real
bind. He gets back about three-thirty.''

Elaine looked at Jimmy who looked back at her with
a similar heartbreaking expression on his face. She
knew the office had their weekly meeting at two
o'clock, but it never took longer than an hour, so she
didn't foresee a problem. Even if it went longer, she
would just excuse herself. With Burt on a parenting

priority—and attracted to Ruth Naomi—he wouldn't object. And if he did, that was too bad. She would just have to leave.

She smiled at father and son. "Sure. Just tell me how to get to your school, and I'm there."

Jimmy relaxed. He might not like her that much, but he wasn't averse to a ride from her.

That settled, dinner went well. They even all traded portions of their dinners for a taste, something the kids actually liked. By the time Ross kissed her at the door, Elaine was feeling very, very good about herself.

Armed with directions to Jimmy's school, Elaine went into her meeting first, determined to watch her time.

"We've got a problem," Burt said, as soon as everyone was seated around the conference table. "Dall Computers has lodged a complaint about our new criteria. They say that our current contract with them holds them exempt from meeting the criteria. Apparently there's a clause that says the terms are nonnegotiable for future use."

"Wait a minute," Elaine exclaimed. "That was for that contract, so they couldn't come back at a later date and provide less because of future changes in their product line."

"That's the call I got from them," Burt said, thrusting his chin out, a clear signal that he was angry. "If we attempt to impose the criteria on them, they threaten to sue for restraint of trade."

He looked directly at Elaine, accusing her with his expression. She gazed back, refusing to show any of her inner anxiety. Dammit, she and Ross hadn't caused this problem. Dall Computers was causing the problem, by hanging their hat on something vague that was never meant to apply to future contracts for different needs. But she knew Burt, and Burt would not only impose the nonfraternization rule again, but he would take it five steps further and make it for the life of the contract. Ridiculous as it was, the man would do it. He was tough and he was fair, something upon which he prided himself and built his business reputation.

"I know they've come into the industry and blown everything out of the water with their bottom-line prices," Tom interjected. "Maybe they don't like it that their competitors are fighting back with innovative service."

Good point, Elaine thought, although she was worried for Ross. If she didn't fight here for what they had built, his company would lose any chance at the job. Or she would lose her job because she couldn't see herself walking away from Ross.

The discussion went round and round, bouncing from the audacity of Dall Computers to the minutia of legal phrasing. To her surprise, Burt never once mentioned what had caused their criteria to be established in the first place. Everyone, even Burt, realized that the criteria had a terrific foundation in common sense for their company's future. No one, not even Burt, wanted to see it dropped, so the ideas were fast and furious over how to handle Dall's demand. Ultimately, Data, Ink, was in the right, but the computer giant could throw legal action after legal action that would cost the company millions to defend. That was the other side of the coin: right as it had been to establish a general criteria to be met by suppliers, was it worth the hassle?

Elaine's head spun by the time the meeting broke up, and even then everyone hung out, still talking about the situation.

Burt snagged her finally, and he said, "I'm still not sure whether to shoot you or me or both of us over this."

"As long as you're not sure," she replied, smiling ruefully. "How can they get away with this? You know that if we back down, we will set the tone and give them an iron fist to smash every company that they deal with."

"I know." Burt's mouth set in a grim line, the way it had been for most of the long meeting. "Dammit, we need a solution. Look, it's late. I'm starving. How about we go out to dinner and continue the discussion—"

"Oh, my god!" Elaine screamed, realizing the time. She shot out of the room and ran for her car, then had to run back to her office to get her purse and keys.

Outside, the darkening sky told her it was way past three-thirty. Even past four-thirty. How could she have been so self-absorbed in the crisis that she never once looked at her watch? How could she have forgotten a child? How could she have been so incredibly stupid?

She drove like a madwoman over to Jimmy's school, even getting lost once on the way. When she finally arrived, only two cars sat in the parking lot. Her heart sank. She raced into the building—or tried to. The front doors were locked. Crying and cursing her stupidity for attempting to take care of a child, Elaine banged on the glass, desperate for anyone inside to let her in.

She was about to give up when a woman emerged from an inside door on the left. Elaine cried in relief that someone had heard her.

"Let me in!" she shouted. "I have to pick up a kid!"

The woman opened a door a few inches. "All the children have gone home."

"No! He couldn't have! I was supposed to pick him up." Elaine wiped at the tears on her face, trying to get some semblance of propriety for herself.

The woman frowned, then smiled. "You must be here for Jimmy Steadwell. He's gone."

"Gone!" Elaine's panic welled up in full force again. "He *can't* be."

"He is," the woman confirmed. "His father picked him up about fifteen minutes ago."

"But...but his father was at a meeting," Elaine replied in confusion.

"Yes, my secretary called his beeper number when Jimmy was the only one left from the field trip." The woman added, "I'm the principal, Dr. Berryman. Don't worry, he's safe and sound."

"I can't believe this happened," Elaine said, thinking of her terrible parenting skills.

"Don't worry about it too much," the woman soothed, sounding exactly like an elementary teacher reassuring a flustered first-grader. "Parents have gotten trapped before and missed a pickup. At least you're here for him. I've had one or two totally irresponsible ones who just haven't bothered and simply expect someone will get their kid home, even if it's me. And it has been."

Elaine didn't feel any better. She had failed in the simple task of picking a child up from school, an everyday event in the lives of parents everywhere.

Once again her domestic shortcomings were pointed out in significant detail.

"HOW ARE YOU FEELING, Jimmy?"

Ross asked the question from the pit of his stomach,

where fear lay that his child had been scarred for life from the past few hours.

"Okay. Can I have that cupcake?"

"Sure."

Pushing said cupcake over to the boy, Ross relaxed a little at his son's nonchalant attitude about being accidentally left at school. By Elaine. Who was at a meeting!

He knew that because he'd called her office from his meeting, and Tina had told him. Never had he been so angry as he had in those few seconds of the phone call. Tina offered to page her, but Ross told her no, preferring at that point to retrieve his son himself. His own meeting had been blown out of the water, a major contract right down the tubes, but he hadn't hesitated. Jimmy came first.

"Daddy, you look sad," Ariel said, leaning against his leg.

"Do I?" He wasn't surprised. He felt sad. Elaine had warned him she wasn't domestic, but he hadn't thought she would be irresponsible with a child. "Jimmy, are you sure you're okay?"

Jimmy nodded once, intently eating his cupcake. His eyes were on the television, rather than his father. All of a sudden Jimmy laughed, clearly enjoying whatever was happening in the cartoon world.

His son was none the worse for wear.

When the doorbell rang a few minutes later, Ross knew who it was before he answered it. To see Elaine on his doorstep, her face streaked with dried tears, dispersed a lot of his anger but not all.

"Oh, God," she said, fresh tears in her eyes. "Is Jimmy all right?"

Ross nodded, clamping his jaw against an outburst.

"I am so sorry," she added. "God, I am so sorry. I was in a meeting—"

"Yes, I know," he snapped.

She looked startled. "You do?"

"I called your office when the school called me. Why didn't you tell me you had a meeting and couldn't get him? Why say that you could?"

"But I could!" She brushed nonexistent hair off her face. "I did have a meeting, but it was at two and we have it every week. It never lasts longer than an hour so I didn't see any problem with picking Jimmy up from school. Only we had a...problem and the time passed so fast...I wasn't paying attention to the clock...I didn't realize..."

Elaine burst into tears. Ross's heart thawed at her sincerity. It was clear something had happened that had caused her forgetfulness. While not forgivable, it was understandable.

"Can I see Jimmy?" she asked, between sobs. "I want... Oh, God...to apologize."

He stepped back, taking the door with him so she could enter. "He's in the kitchen."

She nodded as she walked past him. Ariel greeted her first.

"'Laine!" The child smiled happily and raced around the table to embrace Elaine's legs. She looked up at Elaine, then frowned. "You been cryin'!"

Elaine nodded as she unwrapped the little girl from her legs to finish the last few steps to Jimmy. "I'm sorry I wasn't there at three-thirty, Jimmy. I didn't forget you, not really."

Jimmy turned from the television and looked at her for a long moment. "Okay."

He shoved the last of the cupcake in his mouth and turned back to the television.

Elaine's expression, half anxious, half bewildered, made Ross chuckle reluctantly. She was as nonplussed as he was by Jimmy's casual attitude. The only good thing was there seemed to be no lasting effects to Jimmy's psyche. Ross promised to watch his son closely, just in case Jimmy was still upset.

"I promise I'll be there next time—" Elaine glanced over at Ross "—if your father ever lets me come pick you up again from school."

"You can pick me up from my school when I go," Ariel said. "I'm going soon. My daddy says."

"Every day I say," Ross muttered, knowing he told his daughter so, whenever he was at his most frustrated and exhausted. Out loud he said, "We won't worry about that now."

"Have you all had dinner yet?" Elaine asked. "I'd like to take you out if you haven't."

"To where?" Jimmy asked suspiciously.

"Chuck E. Cheese's."

"I'll get my coat." Jimmy raced out of the room, his television program forgotten. Ariel ran after him.

"That's one way to keep him from watching too much TV," Ross commented, while turning off the kitchen set.

"Is it okay?" Elaine asked. "To take you all to dinner to make up for this afternoon's disaster? I should have asked you first, I know."

Ross sighed. "You're trying to buy the kids' approval again."

"At least I'm not doing it with the ballet."

He laughed again, his anger finally dissipated. Hard facts didn't, however. He saved the discussion of them

until after the meal, while the kids played in the restaurant's various activities area. Ross kept a watchful
eye on them.

"Elaine, it wasn't good what happened today."

"I know. Ross, my heart dropped down to my shoes
when I realized how late it was. I had myself all primed
to watch the clock, but the time just slipped by. What
I thought was a few minutes was an hour. I flew over
to that school but you had already been there and got
him. I have never felt so bad in my life." She paused,
then asked, "How much did leaving your meeting
screw it up?"

"Enough. The group manager wasn't happy that I
was out of there like a shot." He tilted his head. "That
account's probably gone to us."

"I'm sorry," she murmured, looking ready to cry all
over again. Her emotional state was clear from her
barely touched pizza.

"Eat your pizza," he said. "We'll all get over it."

She picked at the cheese with her forefinger. "Will
we?"

"I don't know," he admitted more truthfully.
"Jimmy will. Hell, the kid acts as though it happens
to him every day. Maybe that's not a bad thing right
now. But I'm concerned, Elaine."

"I told you I was no good with kids."

"You're better than you think." That was true
enough. Ariel adored her, and Jimmy was neutral about
her. Considering the child remembered his mother's
illness and loss, that was a light-year jump to acceptance. This incident troubled him deep inside, however,
as if he had had an omen that she would never adjust
to a domestic side. Maybe she subconsciously forgot
about Jimmy today to prove her self-condemnation was

right. Finally he added, "It was just a scary thing for Jimmy. And for me. I thought something happened to you at first."

"I know. Can I talk with the people from that meeting?" she asked. "Maybe if I got them to understand that you had arranged everything and had to leave through my fault, they would be more understanding."

"No, it's okay." But it hadn't been good, abruptly shutting down the presentation halfway through it. He would have been better off changing the meeting date even though he'd changed it before.

"I'd like to talk to them. I really would."

He shrugged. "Don't worry about it."

She was silent for a long moment, the sadness in her normally ebullient face breaking his heart. He wanted nothing more than to wrap his arms around her and make the sadness go away.

Jimmy raced by their table, on his way to the indoor jungle gym. The boy grinned hugely, every muscle in his body exuding happy energy. He was fine, perfectly fine.

Suddenly guilt shamed Ross that he was being harder on Elaine than she deserved. People made mistakes, had accidents, weren't perfect. He knew he'd stretched the time himself to pick up Jimmy from school, just to get in an appointment. Just a few minutes—ten, maybe fifteen at the most—but never as long as today. And if he were truthful, he would have to bear some blame because he asked Elaine at the last minute. Picking up a son from school should have been a first priority arrangement, not an afterthought.

Despite the rationalization, he still couldn't get rid of his troubled feelings about the whole thing.

When they called Jimmy and Ariel over to get ready

to leave, the boy enthusiastically chatted about the fun he'd had. Ariel, not to be outdone, insisted Elaine carry her out of the restaurant.

"This is better than that ballet junk, Elaine," Jimmy said.

Elaine laughed. "I'm so glad you liked it."

"Well...I liked all those Christmas lights, remember?"

"I do. I'll keep this place in mind."

"Yeah. Tomorrow night, for dinner."

Ross smiled at the exchange. If Elaine kept feeding him like this, the boy would forgive her anything. And if Jimmy would forgive her, then maybe he should, too. It was his own food for thought on the drive home.

When she would have left the house after dropping them off, he stopped her. "Stay."

She looked at him, her gaze enough to melt him on the spot.

"Stay," he repeated, slipping his arm around her waist and pulling her to him. He nibbled her earlobe, loving the sweet taste of her sensitive flesh.

"Ross." Her breath was catchy and hot against his cheek. Her fingers tightened against his chest. "You were so upset.... I thought—"

"Let's stop doing that," he whispered in her ear.

"What?"

"Thinking. Let's feel instead."

She chuckled as his hand covered her breast. "You're already doing that."

He could feel her nipple harden under her clothes. "I know."

She made love to him with a purity that broke his

heart. Her eagerness to please him held an urgency that he would never forget.

Yet in the aftermath, he couldn't shake the uneasiness he had about their relationship. Something had changed today, something irretrievable.

Chapter Twelve

Elaine wished she could bask in the aftermath of luxurious lovemaking, but deep within her was an emptiness. Even as she lay against Ross's side, she knew things had changed between them.

Yet they made love to each other with an intensity that seared through every part of her. She couldn't get enough of him during the night, nor he of her. She felt unworthy, inadequate, and all of that had culminated yesterday when she missed picking up Jimmy.

"I love you," she said, meaning it but knowing love wasn't enough.

He rubbed her arm. "I love you, too."

She suddenly realized that in the middle of all the other things, she'd never told him the crisis that had delayed her. Whatever was decided would affect him.

"Dall Computers has threatened to file suit against us for the criteria—"

Ross bolted upright in the bed, taking her with him. "What!"

She couldn't help laughing a little as she extricated herself from his embrace. "Let a girl know when you're going to break her in two like that."

"Sorry." He rubbed her back, finding it unerringly in the dark. "Why are they threatening a suit?"

"They say they have a current contract that does not require the criteria and that the contract is nonnegotiable for future use."

"Hell, everybody's got that one so the price can't be jacked up a year later on the same job. But this is a new project, nothing to do with any current one they have. How can they think they can get away with it?"

"Because they're Dall."

"What's Data, Ink, going to do?"

Elaine shrugged. "Right now, panic. We know they can follow through on their threats, and it becomes a contest to see whose lawyers get richer before someone cries 'uncle' and goes for a settlement. We're the test case for this really, because if Dall gets away with it, then they'll be so powerful they'll dictate contract terms for the future."

"They'll wipe out their competitors by forcing everybody to go from contract to contract with them," Ross said. "I believe that's restraint of trade."

"Mmm. So it is. I'll be sure and tell Burt. The other thing is if he pulls the criteria, then the nonfraternization policy goes back into effect."

Ross didn't say anything at first. Finally he settled them both back on the bed. "No wonder you got wrapped up in that meeting."

"That's nice of you to say, but it's no excuse," she replied, feeling awful all over again. Despite Jimmy's easy attitude and chatter with her, she couldn't stop berating herself for not being there when he needed her.

"It's more understandable," he told her. "So it's

very possible that RP could be cut out before we even start.''

She couldn't deny it. Everything depended on Burt. That this only pointed up why the burden of decision shouldn't be on one person wasn't lost on her. If they had a group vote in place to begin with, they would have a decision that at least reflected a majority of the managers. She could also foresee where nothing would get done if they dawdled, whereas one person could move everything forward with a word. Burt had done it often enough.

"Ross, I think if RP came in tomorrow with a written acceptance of all the criteria, showing how it will be met by the company, you would throw Dall a doozy," she said, hoping he would take up the suggestion. "RP is a major player in the industry. If you come onboard without hesitation, other competitors will. I'm sure of that."

"They could leave us hanging out there to dry," he commented, sighing.

"I'm betting they won't. They'll see this for Dall's bully tactics. I think people are waking up to the fact that while they get a terrific price, they're also getting inadequacy in certain areas with Dall. This might be a desperation move on their part to retain their strength."

"And there's no better place to start than with Data, Ink, another major player in the game. I'll talk to my people tomorrow."

"Good." She smiled to herself. At least she was competent in one area. Only it was the wrong one on a personal level with Ross.

She wanted him to tell her that everything was all right now, that she was forgiven. Ross might call it "understandable," but she couldn't forgive herself for what happened. She had failed. Yesterday had been her first true test with kids, and she had failed Ross as well as Jimmy.

Why had she tried for something that just wasn't in her nature? Didn't her mother cook all her meals so she wouldn't be the Ally McBeal of the computer industry?

"Don't worry about it," Ross said.

She thought he could read her mind, then realized he was talking about the criteria mess. She noticed he never said anything regarding what would happen if Burt demanded they break up their relationship. She wanted to ask about it but was afraid.

Somehow she slept, and in the morning when she woke, it was too late for her to leave without the children seeing her. Ariel was first to comment, after she left Ross's bedroom, fully dressed from the night before.

"How'd you get here?" the little girl asked with a puzzled frown. Her nightgown was a tribute to a recent Disney movie. Little red dragons were everywhere over pink plaid.

"I...stayed over night," Elaine said. "I hope that's okay."

"Sure. Where ja sleep? In Daddy's room?"

Elaine nodded, wondering what to say and how to say it.

"Next time you sleep in my room. 'Kay?"

Elaine smiled. "Sure."

Jimmy came out of his bedroom just then. He rubbed his eyes and looked at her. "Hi, Elaine."

"Good morning, Jimmy," she said formally, and feeling like an idiot that she did.

"I gotta go." And off he went to the bathroom.

While Elaine felt she'd weathered that potential storm, she couldn't help wondering if some super-woman would have handled it instinctively better. In fact, she knew some super woman would because said superwoman would have had a wrist alarm watch to ensure she was up and out of the house before causing anyone a moral dilemma. But not her.

At breakfast, the kids were normal, chatting with her, seeming to accept her. She dished out cereal and milk, something she could handle. But she felt herself at a distance from Ross and his family, as if a glass wall stood between them and her. She could look and see and hear, but would never quite fit in.

"Can I go to Mark's house after school tomorrow?" Jimmy asked, after gulping down his orange juice.

"How are you getting there?" Ross asked.

Jimmy shrugged.

"I'll call his mother tonight and we'll work on it."

Elaine sipped her coffee, but never tasted the brew. She knew she could have volunteered to take the boy and pick him up. She knew Ross could have asked her if she would. Instead, it was clear that she wouldn't be asked. She didn't blame him. She understood it. Rationalizing his lack of response didn't stop the hurt, though.

The moment she pulled into the parking lot of Data, Ink, she felt more grounded, more in sync with what the world wanted from her. She greeted her co-workers who waved or said hello, depending on their current mission's attention requirements. Even Tina was distracted, only waving a greeting while she stared at her computer monitor and typed letters at a furious pace.

A pile of work waited for her, along with a pile of telephone messages. Among them had to be a note that

Ross had called yesterday. Tina logged in everything whether it required a callback or not.

Everything here should gratify her abilities and her sense of self-worth. Instead, Elaine laid her head down on the desk and cried.

ROSS LOOKED AT THE DINNER, clearly bought at the supermarket takeout. Roast beef with potatoes and carrots and gravy was far beyond Elaine's novice cooking skills. Although disappointed, he refrained from saying anything. He only wanted Elaine to continue to try her wings in the kitchen. That she hadn't was discouraging.

Yet he only had to look at her and he wanted her so badly. The mixed feelings were getting to him.

"I hate this meat," Ariel announced as she sat down at the table.

"No, you don't," Ross said automatically, while cutting the meal into kiddie-size pieces for her.

"I do, Daddy," the little girl insisted. "My tummy makes a funny noise and I putt-putt out the back."

"She does, Dad," Jimmy confirmed.

Elaine giggled. She looked genuinely amused and not at all offended, but above all she didn't look sad. "My dad says the same thing about roast beef."

"Really?" Wide-eyed, Ariel turned to Ross. "Daddy, do *you*—"

"Just eat the potatoes and carrots," Ross interrupted. "That'll be good enough."

"'Kay," Ariel agreed, popping a piece of potato in her mouth.

"How was your time at Mark's house?" Elaine asked Jimmy.

Even though she looked interested, Ross could tell she overplayed her focus on the boy.

Jimmy shrugged. "I couldn't go."

"Mark's mother couldn't bring him home," Ross explained. He tousled Jimmy's hair. "But Mark's coming over to play on Saturday."

"Yeah," Jimmy said, still clearly smarting over losing out on the current day's play.

Elaine said, "Saturday's better, Jim. You'll have more time with Mark, I would think."

The boy did brighten a little. "Yeah."

"Can you play with me on Saturday?" Ariel asked Elaine.

"I'd love to, but I have to go to work on Saturday," she replied. Looking at Ross, she said, "Big meeting."

"Over the criteria?" he asked.

She nodded. "And what to do about Dall Computers."

Ross shoved a slice of roast beef in his mouth, needing something to occupy him. When he'd taken back her news to his company, everyone there was in a tear over how this would affect their own bid. The criteria didn't bother them as much as Dall pushing to get it canceled did.

"Daddy, you eat too much and you'll putt-putt out the back," Ariel advised.

"Thank you, sweetheart."

Elaine snorted with amusement.

"A kid laughed like that once at our class and his juice shot out his nose," Jimmy told her.

"Really?" Elaine looked impressed. "It must have been disgusting."

"Naa." Jimmy shoved some food in his mouth, half chewed it, then swallowed hard. He finally said, "It was pretty neat."

"You keep eating like that and you'll be passing

your food whole right out your nose," Ross said, reprimanding the boy for not being more careful with his meal.

"Do it!" Ariel exclaimed, practically hopping up and down in her seat.

Elaine chuckled at the notion.

Ross glared at her, not needing her to encourage the boy in that course of action. "Jimmy, don't even think it, because you won't watch television for a week."

"I wasn't gonna do nothing," Jimmy muttered sullenly, taking another forkful and chewing it thoroughly this time. He brightened. "We're gonna have a party at my class for Christmas and Chanukah and Kwaanza so everybody can 'ticipate, Ms. Cochoran says. We have to bring in cupcakes, Dad."

Ross groaned. He'd never get ahead.

"Buy them," Elaine advised. She had a point.

"Can I go to the party?" Ariel asked.

"No," Jimmy said. "It's only for my class."

Ariel's bottom lip trembled. "But I wanna go to the party!"

"Ariel, this is for Jimmy's class. When you go to school, your class will have a party," Ross said, trying to calm the storm before it broke.

"Can't she go, anyway?" Elaine asked. "I remember little brothers and sisters at my class parties."

That did it. Ariel burst into loud wails. "I wanna go! I wanna go!"

"Shut up, baby, you can't!" Jimmy shouted back at her, trying to establish his private territory against the possible Invasion of the Sister.

Ariel leaped out of her chair and began to run around the table. "I wanna go! I wanna go!"

"No! No! No!" Jimmy shouted, his head almost

spinning around three hundred and sixty degrees to make sure Ariel heard him.

"Ross, I don't want to cause trouble," Elaine said loudly over the din, "but can't you call someone to allow Ariel to attend? It doesn't seem fair to me that the little ones are cut out—"

"Enough!" Ross roared.

Ariel squeaked and nearly fell on her face as she abruptly stopped her racing.

Elaine looked horrified. Ross patted her hand in comfort. "Not you."

Elaine relaxed a little.

"Sit down, young lady," Ross said more calmly, having everyone's undivided attention.

Ariel squeezed slowly into her chair, as if trying to make herself as small as possible from her father's wrath. Her tear-streaked face looked stricken, whether from the bad party news or the anger that followed, was hard to tell.

"Tell her, Dad," Jimmy said encouragingly.

Ross glared at Jimmy. "That's enough from you, as well. Any more screaming and yelling, and people are going into the thinking chair."

"There is no thinking chair here," Jimmy said.

"I'll make one, son."

"'Kay," the boy said sullenly.

Ross continued his list of great expectations. "We will not discuss this any further, and there will be no comments about this to each other. Do you understand, James and Ariel?"

The two children nodded.

"Okay. Drink your milk and eat your dinner—"

"But not the meat," Ariel clarified.

"Eat!" Ross ordered.

When his children had picked up their forks and applied themselves to their meals again, he sighed inwardly, knowing it wouldn't do for the kids to see his relief. No parent should reveal how close he was to losing the situation.

He happened to look Elaine's way at that moment. She glanced at him, then shoveled food into her mouth. "I'm eating, I'm eating!"

He tried not to smile or chuckle, but he could feel the grin spreading across his face. He laughed. "I sound like the bellowing bear, don't I? Sometimes you have to do that to get a kid's attention."

She smiled. "I'll file that away for reference."

"Dad…" Jimmy began.

"Don't," Ross said, sobering.

"But I just want more milk."

"Me, too," Ariel said, holding out her full glass.

"Even *I* think you can have that, too," Elaine said, getting milk. She refilled Jimmy's glass and put a dollop in Ariel's.

Progress, he thought. But was it enough?

"WE'RE NOT BACKING OFF our criteria."

Everyone at the meeting cheered Burt's announcement. The CEO grinned, looking like the shark he was. "They ticked me off, I admit it. But we're taking a stand because it's good business to do so."

"All right!" someone called out from around the packed conference table.

"I informed Dall late last night that we needed a fax this morning by ten on how they intended to meet the criteria for their project bid. If we didn't have one, we would assume they were withdrawing. They weren't happy, especially when I pointed out their contract interpretation was restraint of trade.''

"Will we be in court?" Elaine asked.

"It's possible," Burt said, looking unworried. He nodded to a man at his left. "At least it gives Roger here something to do besides vetting clauses and SEC laws."

"They file on us, we file with Justice on their attempts at a monopoly. Justice is breathing down several software companies necks at the moment." Roger looked smug.

"What the hell," Burt said happily. "It's only money."

Elaine thought Burt looked very pleased with himself. She wondered if he found the corporate fight a distraction from his divorce fight. She also wondered if he finally made it to first base with Ruth Naomi.

She wanted to tell him hitting home runs wasn't a guarantee to happiness. Her involvement with Ross seemed more and more as if it only had a sexual base. Once again, she had been on completely the wrong wavelength, Ariel's outburst the newest case in point.

Everyone around the boardroom table began to discuss various approaches and repercussions. Elaine once again felt in her element. Strategies were brought up, shot down or filed way for future consideration.

She contributed five or six, inspired by the suggestions of others. Corporate crises were her specialty; domestic ones clearly her nemesis.

At 10:05 Burt's secretary rushed in with a pile of papers.

"It came," she announced. "Ten minutes ago. I made copies as you wanted, Mr. Langdon."

"Thanks."

Burt perused them quickly, then passed them out. "Well, folks, it's criteria specs not a court summons. Looks like Dall is playing ball."

"For the moment," Roger the attorney commented, his expression almost crestfallen.

Elaine grinned. When she got her copy of Dall's fax, she read through it, picking out the important points. The committee had had copies of RP Computers' bid and criteria, as well as several others.

They discussed Dall's options to meet the criteria as well as the others. Eventually Burt brought it to a halt, saying, "These criteria were designed to take any personal bias out of the decision. Before we vote, I want you all not to feel pressured by the boss, so I'll step outside while you have any last discussion regarding the companies involved in the bidding." Burt nodded toward the door. "Elaine, will you join me?"

"Yes, of course." She rose and walked to the conference door, Burt following her. Before he opened the door itself, he said to the room, "Ladies and gentlemen, get us the best deal."

In the corridor, they walked together to the nearest desks and sat down. The conference room was off the secretarial pool, so the little cubicles in the sales department were nowhere to be seen. Just an acre of desks.

"Whenever I pass this area, I think of that movie *9 to 5*," Burt said, lifting a picture and looking at the family displayed by the desk's occupant. "I make sure I don't say a word that would offend because I don't want to be shot at, hog-tied, roasted or poisoned and launched out of my office chair."

Elaine laughed. "We're only three floors up." She

leaned over the desk at which she sat. "You didn't sound ready to fight last week. What happened?"

Burt shrugged. "I got tired of getting shoved around by lawyers and figured I'd shove back."

She grinned. "Dall doesn't stand a chance."

"Hell, I knew that the moment they faxed the criteria requirements this morning." Burt smiled slightly. "I wondered if I had a fight up until then. Oh, they'll rattle their sabers, and they'll push for concessions in other ways, but they know they didn't have a leg to stand on."

"They picked the wrong company to bully." She glanced over to the closed doors. "What do you think they'll decide?"

"Worried about Ross?" Burt asked.

"I won't lie," she replied. "I'd like to see him get the contract. He's worked very hard to give us what we want."

"Oh, so you don't just have the hots for him." Burt grinned.

"I'll have to complain to his mother."

Elaine laughed at the ludicrous suggestion.

Burt grew serious. "You're a lucky woman, Elaine. He's a good guy, actually helped me a little with my kids."

As Burt talked about her good fortune, Elaine wished he were right. But she wasn't lucky. Even when she found a man who stirred her beyond all reason, who made her feel loved and special in many ways, she still couldn't get things right. She couldn't even pick up a kid at the right time from school, that's how bad she was.

And if they continued their relationship, she could

only see it getting worse. After all, life was one domestic crisis after another.

The conference doors opened and they were waved back inside. Roger, the attorney, passed out little ballots he'd made, obviously not letting a legal moment slip by him. Each one had their individual name printed on it, clearly having been made beforehand. The democratic process only went so far before the corporate process overcame it. Elaine made her vote, folded her paper over and passed it back. When everyone had turned in his vote, Roger put on his reading glasses and counted them.

"RP Computers received a unanimous vote," Roger announced.

With a yelp of joy, Elaine shot up from the chair as if she'd been launched from it. Her happiness overwhelmed her and she raced from the room, laughter following her. She moved through the corridors like lightning to her office, not wanting a single disruption while she made her call.

When she got Ross at home, she shouted into the telephone receiver, "You got it!"

"Yes!" he shouted back. "We beat Dall?"

"Everyone beat Dall!" she exclaimed, thrilled for him. "Ross, you worked so hard for RP, and this is so wonderful. I couldn't be happier for you."

"Hey. You got us there, honey. So when do we meet to discuss implementation?"

"Tonight," she said. "Let's go out to dinner and have champagne. We both deserve it, I think."

"I think you're right. I'll get my mother to babysit."

"Burt won't be happy," Elaine said, giggling.

"That's his problem." Ross was quiet for a moment

before he added, "I know things have been...strained between us lately, but let's forget that and move on."

She smiled, elation running through her veins so hard and so enthusiastically that nothing else could penetrate her thinking. He still wanted to be with her—that was all she needed to hear. "That's a wonderful idea."

A fresh start. Maybe that was what they needed.

ELAINE CHATTERED AWAY all through dinner at a cozy Italian restaurant on Princeton's Main Street. The upscale decor and isolated tables provided a good deal of privacy in the open dining room. The light from the table candle reflected off the snowy-white linens and bathed Elaine's face in a soft golden glow.

Her smile was beguiling, promising him the world. Her skin was satin soft, making his fingers ache to touch her. Her conversation was all business, oddly stimulating his own and his own admiration for her. Her happiness at their victory fed his own. He wanted her, right on the spot.

"What?" she asked, obviously seeing something in his expression.

"You," he said. "I was just watching you."

She smiled. "Really?"

"Don't sound so surprised," he said. "You know what you do to me."

"I know what you do to me," she replied.

He was right to want to keep trying with their relationship. Doubts crept in, but he pushed them out. She was vivacious and wonderful in so many ways. The problems with her domestic side could be worked out.

"Can we get out of here?" he asked. "I want to do some real celebrating."

She laughed and rose from the table. "Ross, you're not getting up."

He leered. "Wanna bet?"

She grinned when he rose to his feet. "You are a dirty old man."

"I'm a *rich* dirty old man," he said, throwing money down on the table and taking her elbow. "Thanks to you and Burt."

"Don't thank me. You turned in the great proposal. And don't thank Burt. He nearly dumped you out over me. I think he's grateful now that he was saved from himself."

Ross grinned. "Now my mother's off the hook, too, with him."

"I don't know about that. He believes in pursuit."

"So do I," he whispered, when they stopped to retrieve their coats.

He drove her to her house, Elaine snuggled against his side. He felt the rightness of her with him. The satisfaction of her simple companionship reached deep within his heart. He didn't feel alone anymore when he was with her. Yes, she'd made a very bad mistake, but he would bet she never made it again.

A part of him immediately took the odds. He thrust out his jaw and forced it away. He didn't ask her to drive Jimmy to his friend's house because she had to work. An emergency was one thing, but going to a friend's house wasn't. He'd told himself that over the past few days, and he believed it. He had to.

The moment her front door shut behind them, they were all over each other with an urgency he couldn't have described if he tried. He didn't have breath to. Every kiss, every touch, just went straight through him, the need for her so great and so much more than celebrating a shared victory.

Her mouth was like fire on him everywhere, as if she were branding him or absorbing him or doing both. He loved the way she made him feel. He loved her.

Even as he entered her, even as she surrounded him with her own flesh, he sensed himself struggling for something that just wasn't fixable between them. He hated himself as he loved her with his body and his soul.

But all the business deals weren't enough to cure what was going wrong between them. Was there anything that would?

Chapter Thirteen

"What should I get Ariel and Jimmy for Christmas?"

Elaine asked the question as she and Ross sat at the coffee bar in his mother's store late Sunday afternoon. She wanted to be perfect now, no mistakes to mar this second chance.

Suddenly the perfect thing popped into her head, a full-blown vision of Jimmy and Ariel happily playing with her gift for years and years to come.

She looked at Ross and knew he'd hate it. Forget the puppy, she told herself.

"I don't know," he said having no clue that she needed guidance or she would get the gift she'd just thought of. "Anything you want to give them is fine."

Her blood pressure shot up fifty points at the vague answer. "Ross, you know damn well that if I get them something you don't approve of, you'll be very unhappy with me. And you'll make sure I know it."

"You make me sound like Critical Father Knows Best," he complained.

"I feel like Dummy Girlfriend Knows Least," she replied, her sense of elation fading as quickly as it had appeared. In the aftermath of lovemaking, she fought that little corner of emptiness that said no matter how compatible in bed they were, no matter how compatible in business they were, she was still a failure where it counted.

"Hi, guys."

Ross's brother, Micah, pulled up a chair and sat down at their little table. He set an oversize coffee cup, filled to the brim, on the fake marble top. His eyes were bleary and his hair went every which way. A good day's stubble stood out on his lower face.

Ross tucked his chin down and eyed his brother. "Gig last night?"

"You have no idea." Micah rubbed one eye with the heel of his hand, then snorted in clear disgust. "Ross, my brother, my friend. What did I ever ask for in life?"

"A bottle of tequila and a hot woman?"

Micah chuckled, his voice raspy. "Absolutely. Now get serious."

"I thought I was." Ross frowned. "You wanted to be the next Grand Funk Railroad."

"Bingo. Get a big break and outsell the Beatles at Shea Stadium. Instead, I play clubs up and down the mid-Atlantic States. I even have a damn good following at times."

"Are you lamenting your life?" Elaine asked, curious.

"Hell no, honey. I'm lamenting last night. We got discovered."

Ross straightened. "What!"

"A guy from Sony Records...*the* talent guy from Sony East goes slumming in a club down by A.C., where we're playing. We had some of our new tunes up, and he went nuts for them. He offered us a contract on the spot, studio time to cut a demo and all the push the record company could give.''

Elaine shrieked with happiness for Micah. She threw her arms around his neck and hugged him, bussing him on the cheek for good measure. ''That's wonderful.''

Ross grinned and slapped Micah on the back. ''Nobody deserves it more than you.''

''Yeah, that's it.'' Micah sounded as morose as a guy could get. ''We sat around and talked, the guys and me afterward, about it. We've seen bands get this kind of break before and suddenly they're not what they were. The company cleans them up, puts an image on them, fosters it—you've got to foster it—and then somebody's head gets too swollen and you're breaking up a great band. I've only seen one guy, one band, stay true to themselves and that's Southside Johnny and the Asbury Dukes. They've been offered breaks, even got in a movie or two on cameos, but they turned down record deals when they saw what it would take out of them. It's killing me.''

''You guys are going to walk away from it,'' Ross said.

''We already did,'' Micah replied, then drank down the huge cup of coffee. He grinned widely. ''Damn, but it was great!''

''But...but...'' Elaine sputtered, shocked that anyone would be offered the world they wanted on a silver platter and would refuse to take a bite. ''How could you pass up a terrific opportunity like that? Especially if it's one you've wanted all your life.''

''Amazing, ain't it?'' Micah's grin nearly split his face. ''We love playing the little clubs. We don't get our original music rejected before it has a chance to be out there. Best of all, we get to be ourselves, a garage band that's having a great time. When the offer finally came to us, we all realized it hadn't been our dream for a long time now.''

Elaine had trouble assimilating what Micah said. Wasn't a big-name contract a crowning achievement for a band?

Micah grew serious as he warmed to his point. ''Not everyone makes the majors, Elaine. Not everyone *should.* Look at little brother here. Did he ever tell you he was offered a big job with IBM, straight out of college?''

''No.'' Elaine turned to Ross.

Ross shrugged. ''I would have been swallowed alive in that place. Probably been downsized out of there, too, eventually. I knew I was better off where I was.'' He laughed. ''Although they went bankrupt after a few years. I'd already left them for RP by that time, for more benefits and latitude. I'll never make a million a year, but I'll never kill myself at it, either.''

''I guess I understand,'' Elaine said finally.

Micah chuckled. ''And I understand astrophysics. Hell, I don't even understand what I did. It just felt right.''

''Have you told Mom?'' Ross asked.

Micah snorted. ''What? And have her bounce off the walls?''

''It's great news. She'd be happy for you.''

''I know, but she'll also push me and the guys to take it.'' Micah stood. ''Well, I better get going. I've got a gig tonight. Another club, another show. It's probably the biggest mistake of my life, but what the hell.''

When he left, Elaine turned to Ross. ''I'll never get it.''

"He does, and that's all that matters."

She felt as if she were being told something, that Micah's choice and Ross's understanding of it had a message for her. Micah was a Peter Pan kind of guy while Ross was a Dudley Doright, and yet they were on the same ground, while she couldn't even find the dirt.

Ross gave her carte blanche for the children's gifts, but he didn't mean it.

She was more lost than ever.

ROSS LOOKED AROUND his house, at the decorations he was supposed to put up, and knew the holidays would be very tough on his family.

Elaine tried draping a piece of garland across his fake mantel in the living room. As soon as she let it go, it fell off.

"Hell," she muttered.

"Hell," Ariel repeated, helping her pick it up.

Elaine giggled, validating Ariel's misbehavior, then said, "No, no, Ariel. That's a bad word."

"'Kay," Ariel replied.

Ross wondered if his daughter was thoroughly confused with the conflicting reactions on Elaine's part. He'd worry about it later. Jimmy sat on a chair, his expression solemn as he watched Elaine and Ariel retry to hang the garland. He knew what Jimmy was feeling. Ever since Barbara had passed away, the holidays hadn't been the same.

When the kids went to bed a little later, he sat down with Elaine on the sofa and said, "I don't know what to do about Christmas anymore."

"What do you mean?" she asked.

"This house is a pretty sad place at Christmas," he

replied. "Ariel doesn't remember much, but I can still see pain in Jimmy's face. It's going to be very hard for them, him especially."

"Oh."

He was silent for a while.

"I should be helping you with this," Elaine said, her voice low. "I know I should be, but I don't know what to do, either. I don't know anything about what to do for kids who are hurting. I never even noticed that Jimmy was upset. I'm hopeless."

He meant to disagree with her, that she wasn't hopeless, but he hesitated for just a moment, his darker, doubtful side concurring with her assessment of herself.

"This isn't going to work, is it, Ross?" she asked, turning to him. Her eyes were wide and filled with tears. "We can try. We can be great in the bedroom and the office. But here, where it really counts with all the little things kids and households need, we aren't compatible. It's been bumpy between us lately, and I can tell it'll get worse, not better. I think now I understand your brother's point. Know your limitations. I've been trying to stretch out of mine and it's been making all of us unhappy. Maybe we ought to stop this thing before we turn nasty with each other. I couldn't stand that."

"Elaine." He felt as if she had hit him in the stomach with a power punch. His chest was tight, and his brain hurt as it tried to assimilate her words. She was breaking up with him.

"Please," she said, waving a hand. "Don't even try to tell me you haven't seen the inevitable between us. We're better off facing it now than hurting each other—and the kids—even more, later."

He couldn't deny it. Out of respect for her, he didn't

try. So why didn't he feel a twinge of relief in all the pain? Why did his heart protest so much underneath it all?

"I love you," he whispered.

"I love you," she said.

But it wasn't enough, and neither tried to sell the other that it was.

He reached out and touched her cheek, feeling the softness, the rightness of her flesh against his fingers. He couldn't imagine not touching her again, not having her in his bed, not laughing with her over things. If only a miracle suddenly appeared that could throw her common sense right out the window.

"The kids," he said. "They've had enough trauma at the holidays. It would be even harder on them to lose you right now."

"Oh, God. I wouldn't want that." Tears spilled over, and she wiped them away with the back of her hand. "I could be around until after the holidays."

He leaped on it, anything to keep her with him for a little longer. "That would be good."

"Maybe...maybe we should do something special for them," she said. "I know. Why not go away for Christmas? Like to the Caribbean or something?"

He opened his mouth to tell her how ridiculous it was to take little kids to the beach for Christmas, then realized he was about to be Critical Father again. "It's a good idea, but I'm wondering if the kids would worry that Santa Claus wouldn't be able to find them in the sand."

"Oh. I didn't think." She smiled slightly. "I guess I would worry about Santa not finding me... Hey! What about the Pocono Mountains? Reindeer and Santa and snow go together, right?"

He grinned at the association and knew it was something the children would find less strange, but only a little less. The whole notion of not being home for Christmas was alien. He still doubted its practicality, but had to admit it was a solution of sorts. "It's not bad. I even know someone who has a place at the mountains. Marge's daughter."

"Why don't you see if she's not using it?" Elaine suggested. "It would be a place with no memories...for any of us..."

Her voice trailed away. Ross watched the sadness deepen in her eyes. He wished she didn't have the emotion. He wished she didn't need to have the emotion. He didn't want to be civilized about breaking up. Rage shot through him, a small shaft of it only to be extinguished with the knowledge that they were at a stalemate that was unfixable. It was better for all to let it go, than to really hurt each other—and the kids—trying to hold on to something already dying.

He leaned over and kissed her tenderly, gently melding his tongue to hers in search of comfort and love. When he would have eased his mouth away, she pressed her fingers to his cheeks, keeping his kiss to hers. Her lips quested over his with a bittersweetness that broke his heart. He put his arms around her and brought her to him, tasting her mouth, imprinting its uniqueness in his mind forever. Why couldn't a person be all things to another person? Why did there have to be large gaps that were unfillable? He felt as if he were having something precious taken away from him again, and again he couldn't stop it.

They undressed slowly, their hands savoring each other's bodies, poignancy wrapped up in sensuality. Her flesh was soft and warm, and hot and moist. Her body was strong yet fragile. He could break her and break himself against her in the same moment. Their mouths memorized every inch of skin until she was writhing under him, accepting his body within her own, becoming one with him.

Even as he caught her cry of satisfaction with his lips, he felt a burst of hope that faded to a vapor. Love didn't conquer all, it only prolonged the agony.

"YOU'RE WHAT?"

Elaine's mother stared at her, slack-jawed at the idea of her daughter not being home for the holidays. The older woman had brought over the week's meals she'd cooked for her daughter. Elaine felt guilty even looking at them, knowing they were a major contributor to her lack of domestic efficiency.

Elaine raised her chin. "Mom, I'm going to the Poconos with Ross and his family this year. It's not rocket science."

"I know it's not," Mary Baransky said. "I don't like it."

"You'll like this. We're breaking up," Elaine snapped, her voice breaking.

Her mother gaped at her. "You are?"

"Yes. We're going away because it's Christmas and because we both want to give them a nice time before I'm out of the picture."

"I..." Her mother looked stricken. "I don't know what to say. You're hurting."

"Yes, I am." Elaine paused. "Mom, don't hassle me about Christmas. I'm going with Ross."

Her mother nodded. "But what about your father and me? What do we do this Christmas?"

"Mom, you know what? I think you and Dad ought

to go to the Caribbean for the holidays,'' Elaine said. Warming to the idea, she added, ''You both work so hard, why not enjoy yourselves this year? It's not too late. Hey! Think of the warm sand under your feet and the tropical breezes blowing through your hair—''

''Your father's bald.''

''Blowing through his scalp. Think of late nights doing the cha-cha and even later...who knows? You might get lucky.''

''Yeah, if it's not with your father.'' But Mary grinned. ''God, it would be nice to get away.''

''There you go, Mom,'' Elaine said, encouraging the notion. ''You could shop till you drop. Buy Dad a couple of Hurricanes, and he'll carry your packages anywhere. You won't be fighting the mall crowds or making major house renovations just to look like a winter wonderland. Why not let it be just you and Dad again? Like a second honeymoon.''

''Maybe,'' her mother conceded, clearly mulling over the idea.

''And Mom...'' Elaine waited until she had her mother's undivided attention. ''Don't cook me any more meals, okay?''

Her mother gaped. ''What!''

''No more, Mom,'' Elaine said firmly. ''I never learned to cook or do anything domestic because I never had to. I really appreciate all you do, but one thing I've learned in this is that it's time to throw me to the wolves. If you bring me meals or do anything domestic for me, I'll just throw it out.''

Her mother was still protesting Elaine's decision as she left, but Elaine knew she'd done what was best for their mother-daughter relationship. She also bet her best pair of panty hose that her parents would be

booked on a package deal to St. Martin or some other
island before the day was out. Her father wouldn't
know what hit him. She almost smiled at that one.

For herself, however, each day was more dreadful
than the next. She bought Jimmy the latest set of micro
cars so he could hot-rod on the leading edge of kiddie
cars. He would like that, and she felt it was a present
Ross would approve of. For Ariel she bought a singing
stuffed doggie, one famous on kiddie television. Not a
real puppy, but something close enough. And again,
Ross's approval rating for her would be in the black.
Ross was the toughest to buy for, but a puzzle with six
different solutions kept catching her eye. She wished
they had six different solutions to their mismatch, but
she couldn't resist the impulse to get the symbolic gift
for him. Not that she'd ever seen him do a puzzle, but
something took her hand to get out the money for the
thing. She got little things to round out her list for
them, as well.

She sat in her car afterward and cried. She cried
because it was the first and last time she would buy
gifts for them for the holidays. She cried because she
felt a deep satisfaction in the giving, and she would
never have it again with the family she'd come to love.

She wiped her eyes and muttered, "Now I know
why Mom feels so lost this Christmas."

Only her mother was getting on a plane in the morning for Las Vegas with her father. No beach for the
elder Baransky family, just half-naked showgirls and
one-armed bandits. They were ecstatic with their great
travel agency magic and first-class package that cost
them a fortune. Clearly, they were enjoying the very
different Christmas present they were giving each
other.

Elaine never let her lost Christmas feeling show with Ross, however. She had said the words that had started them on this path to finality. She would accept whatever came with a cheerfulness that belied the hurt. Despite her efforts and attempts, she was no good at the greatest job in the world. Not even a Mommy Club could have saved her. Not when she'd forgotten Jimmy at school that day. She had seen her true self on Ross's face, had seen it on Jimmy's and had felt it in her heart. She wasn't right for him and his family. She wasn't right for anyone's.

So she would go through the motions, for them, for their holiday, and then it would be over.

Elaine received the first inkling that all was not well when Ross called her the night before Christmas Eve day.

"We've got a problem," he said.

Her heart dropped as she said, "What is it?"

"That proposal I was working on when I had to leave to get Jimmy..." He said it matter-of-factly, with no blame in his voice. She felt her conscience whip-crack her with it anyway. "It's back on board, but I have to see them tomorrow morning first thing. Or it's off again."

"But it's Christmas Eve!" Elaine protested.

"You're in business, honey. You know Scrooge isn't dead. Not at the level we're at."

She smiled wryly. Corporate types were A people in a B world sometimes.

"I don't expect to be done until late in the afternoon, which really screws things up because I had some shopping still to go."

"You? Mister Organized?" she scoffed, grateful that they could still tease each other even in the disintegra-

tion. That friendliness told her all the more that breaking up was accepted between them, even right to do.
One thing she wouldn't be was his friend. Neither of
them suggested they should be, afterward, and she
hoped neither of them ever would.

"Don't tell The Daddy Club I have no clue," he
said. "I'll never live it down. It looks like we won't
get in much before midnight tomorrow. If at all. Maybe
we shouldn't try this. It's almost a four-hour drive to
the place."

"Ross." She hesitated to make a suggestion, then
plowed ahead. "Ross, look. Why don't I pick up the
kids early tomorrow and go up to the cabin?"

"Oh, I don't know, Elaine."

"I understand," she replied, hurting that he still
didn't trust her and knowing that was the crux of everything. But she wanted the kids to have happy memories of the holidays. That outweighed her pain. "I
promise that I will be very careful with the kids. But I
understand if you're uncomfortable with that."

"No…I… No, you're right. There's no reason why
you guys can't go up early and get things ready."

Elaine panicked for a moment at actually being
given the responsibility, then she took courage. She
would do this and she *wouldn't* make a mistake.
"Don't worry about a thing. I'll stop for lunch with
them on the way. We'll eat, I promise, and not something I make."

He chuckled.

She added, "But this way, the kids will be able to
play in the snow a little on Christmas Eve. We rarely
have snow for Christmas here."

"It'll be a treat. It will also make things easier with

the presents. I can bring all of them up with me when I come.''

''Just like Santa,'' she said.

''I don't think Santa's been driving around with some of them in his car trunk for the past three weeks. Do you know how tough it is to squeeze groceries in the back seat along with two kids and avoid their questions on why I'm doing it?''

No, she thought. She didn't know, and she never would.

BOTH CHILDREN WERE EXCITED when she picked them up the next morning. They gave their father hugs and hardly a backward glance, something that pleased Elaine because it showed they were comfortable with her. She would not fail.

''I wish you weren't going,'' he said as they stood by her open driver's-side door.

''I'll be careful driving,'' she promised Ross.

He set his jaw for a moment and looked away, when his gaze returned, he said, ''That's not why.''

''Oh.'' That he meant it would be their own last time together brought a sudden lump of unshed tears in her throat. She forced it away. ''I'll still be careful.''

He smiled a little, but looked as hurt as she felt. He kissed her goodbye, his mouth lingering, then he kissed her again fiercer and hotter. Elaine got in her car and started the engine. She knew she would never survive this weekend and for her, she would always feel the pain at this time of year.

She no sooner turned onto the northeast extension of the Pennsylvania Turnpike, when large snowflakes fell one by one on her windshield. Jimmy had been singing to the tape of children's songs she'd put in her cassette player, but now he said, "Wow! It's really snowing."

Ariel, who had been silent and probably sleeping, piped up, "Snowing! Can we make a snowman?"

"When we get there," Elaine replied.

"When will we get there?" Ariel asked.

"A while yet."

"I'm hungry and I hafta go to the bathroom," Jimmy said.

"Me, too," Ariel added.

"Me, too, too," Elaine chimed in.

Food and drink and necessities taken care of without too much fuss on anyone's part, Elaine herded them back into the car and on their way again. The snow-flakes turned smaller and denser. She knew the weather report had predicted a few inches of snow, not anything that should be a problem, but she turned on the radio for news, just in case. She was relieved to hear Philadelphia and the surrounding area were still in for those same couple of inches. No problem. In fact, a little snow on Christmas Eve was a perfect omen for giving the children a wonderful holiday, she thought.

They stopped a few more times for small bodies to relieve themselves and each time, the snow seemed a little thicker. But the turnpike was in great shape, so Elaine wasn't worried. When they got off the turnpike at their exit, however, Elaine frowned.

The snow was heavier in the mountains, coming fast and furious. It looked as if it was more than a couple inches—and building. Worse, the storm had those ominous swirling gusts that blinded drivers at times and a biting chill that wormed its way under winter coats. They made a quick bathroom stop. As they walked across the parking lot, Jimmy and Ariel tried to catch snowflakes with their tongues. They were doing a good job of it, too.

"Come on, kids, we've still got a ways to go," she said, while they protested but went before her reluctantly.

In the car, she tried to turn on the news, but Ariel whined for more music. Giving in, Elaine shoved another top-forty hit parade from the Sesame Street Chorus into the cassette player. As the kids sang and chattered with each other, she concentrated on the worsening roads. The tarmac provided little traction as she rode up and down slopes that were becoming dangerously angled. Although the roadway had been plowed, it glistened forebodingly, signaling the onslaught of black ice. Elaine could barely see in front of her, and the plowed road quickly disappeared under a white blanket that was fast becoming thicker than all the mattresses that the princess encountered when she slept on the pea.

"This is lots of snow," Jimmy said too quietly. He was worried.

Elaine tried to dispel his concern. "We're in the mountains. They have snow all the time like this."

But the child was right: it was lots of snow. Much more than she was used to driving in. She knew from the directions that the house was about twenty miles from the turnpike entrance. She had the hand-drawn map the owner had given Ross, but nothing looked exactly how she thought it should. As she drove in more and more confusion, she clocked her odometer. At least it would give her a clue how close she might be. All she saw was trees and snow. She wondered if she should turn around but she knew the return roads were no better than the ones ahead. And they couldn't be too far from the cabin now. Belatedly she turned on the radio, got static, then pushed the Search button until she got something clear. Her heart fell.

In the hours since she'd left home, the snow had stalled against a quick-moving weather front and was now a major blizzard. The Poconos, of which she was smack in the middle, were expecting close to a foot. The announcer had the nerve to cheerfully add that this was great Santa flying weather.

"Oh, God," Elaine murmured, wanting to cry.

The car suddenly spun out from under her, the wheel wildly turning. She locked her grip on it as she realized she must have hit a patch of ice under the snow. Jimmy and Ariel screamed as the car whipped completely around in a three-hundred-and-sixty-degree circle, despite her efforts to control the vehicle. She felt a drop and a bump and a wrench that threw her forward in her seat belt, then back again. Her head banged against the headrest, but not hard enough to hurt. The car stalled, its nose down and its back end up. Elaine sat, numbed for a time until she recognized crying in the distance. The motor was still running. She turned it off, yanked open her seat belt and turned around.

"Are you two okay?" she asked, while searching anxiously for any signs of blood or broken bones.

Just tears flowed from Jimmy and Ariel.

"Hold on," she said, opening her car door. It only moved about halfway in its arc before the bottom end jammed against the ground. Elaine saw the car was in a small ditch that ran alongside the road. God, she thought, she'd never realized it was there, the covering snow leaving only a vague depression.

Gingerly, she squeezed out of the door. Her feet almost slid from under her. She knew whatever water was in the ditch was frozen. She wasn't sure how long her designer boots would have lasted in water. Opening the backdoor as far as it would go, she reached in and hugged both children. As their small arms went around her neck tightly, she felt all the dependency within them—and all the responsibility bestowed on her. They were okay, just shaken. She was over the first hurdle, she thought. No physical injuries.

"I want my daddy!" Ariel wailed.

Me, too, Elaine thought to herself. She knew it might not instill confidence in the kids to hear her say it. But she desperately wished Ross were here.

She disengaged herself from their embrace. "Look, we're kind of stuck for a little while because I can't push the car out of the ditch we're in. But another car will be along soon, and we'll get help then. Okay?"

The two nodded, solemn and tear streaked.

"You are both so brave." She hugged them again. "I'll just sit here next to you and we'll sing songs."

She got in, after removing Ariel's seat belt and sliding her over by Jimmy. She remembered her cell phone and reached over the front, to take it from a cubbyhole in her dash. With the car tipped nose down, she felt as if she was about to fall into the windshield. She tried calling 911, but she got dead air, indicating she was in a bad cell where the signal was weak.

Refusing to worry about it, she cuddled Ariel next to her and patted Jimmy's shoulder for comfort while they waited for a rescue. They sang songs, all the ones they heard all afternoon instead of weather reports. Elaine watched the blizzard swirl and swirl like a fast whirlpool around the car. It grew colder and darker. She prayed for a car to pass.

"I'm cold," Jimmy said.

"I hafta go to the bathroom real bad," Ariel added.

"Where's a damn car?" Elaine muttered to herself.

But a car never came. The kids complained more and more. Finally she climbed into the front seat to start the car for warmth, but it wouldn't start. Instead she wrapped the kids and herself in a quilt she'd brought. She couldn't help with the bladder problem, a more and more urgent one for herself, as well.

"I'm freezing!" Jimmy moaned, his teeth chattering.

"I hafta go!" Ariel wailed.

"Okay, okay. Calm down," Elaine said.

Ariel burst into tears. Jimmy's lip quivered. Patience deserted Elaine faster than an MTV crowd would have deserted the Osmond Brothers. She knew what she had to do.

"Make sure your coats and mittens and hats are on tight," she ordered. "We'll walk to the house. We can't be far."

She checked her own clothing, then opened the car door and got out. She helped Ariel then Jimmy to the ground, grateful both wore boots. She took the quilt for added protection. Wrapping it around herself, she gathered the children under it to keep them close and warm.

The three shuffled off into the night.

"I THOUGHT I'D STOP IN with your presents before I take off for the mountains," Ross said to his mother. He watched the white stuff piling up outside Hardware and Muffins and had heard the reports that the storm was beginning to stall over the area. Elaine and the kids had to be up at the house by now. His own trip would be a little tough, but he'd make it, come hell or high water. Or high snow, he amended.

"Thanks." She eyed the boxes critically. Her store

was closed, but she was waiting there for her friends to gather so they could leave for Atlantic City. The ladies were partying for the holidays. "They're very big and very small. Looks like I get good stuff this year."

"A blender, a mixer and a bright-red bead necklace from Ariel," Ross replied.

His mother chuckled, knowing he was joking. Household things had always been forbidden as gifts. The jewelry, however, was right on the money. It was a hideous thing only a three-year-old could love. His mother would wear it with pride for that reason alone.

"I need a hug," Ruth N. said, giving him one. "Looks like you and Elaine will be snowed in up there. Better hurry, you don't want to miss all that good sex after the kids go to bed."

"Yeah." Ross could hear the lack of enthusiasm in his voice.

So could his mother evidently. "Okay, what's wrong?"

Ross didn't deny Ruth Naomi's perception. "Elaine and I are breaking up after the holidays."

He told his mother his concerns and how both he and Elaine had agreed it wouldn't work.

In answer, his mother hit him, slapped him right on the arm and looked outraged as she did.

"Are you insane?" she demanded, "Elaine is wonderful and she's all the kids can talk about. Ariel doesn't care if she's got a clean shirt or not. Jimmy needs attention, not a perfectly cooked meal. They want someone who cares about them, that's all. She does care. Look at all the effort she's gone to in showing it. The ballet, the toys, the dinners, the running around everywhere with you three. She's tried to be there as much as possible. Just be there for all of you. And you, Mr. Daddy Perfect Club, why can't you take care of clean shirts and home-cooked meals, since you're so big on that? Accept that she's different. Accept that she's good for the kids. And very good for you.''

"But...what about forgetting Jimmy at school?" Ross said, feeling small for bringing it up. But he couldn't get the incident out of his head. It was the thing that lowered the trust between them.

Ruth banged her fist down on the counter. "Then you better disown me because I forgot him earlier this year."

Ross gaped at her. "What!"

Ruth Naomi nodded. "I did, the second week of school. I wasn't used to him going yet and totally forgot I was supposed to pick him up. He was there an hour when Ula Mae reminded me about it. He was crying pretty bad when I got there. I swore him to secrecy and bought him two ice creams, as well as a car set he'd been wanting. He forgave me, and I'm still his best bud, but if anyone traumatized him, I did. Not Elaine. And I'll tell you this, hotshot father, I *never* forgot him again. Neither will Elaine.''

"I can't believe you did that!" Ross began, furious with her for never telling him and bribing his son not to tell, either.

"You can stand here yapping at me straight through Christmas or you can get in your car and get up there and make things right with Elaine again." She took him by the shoulders and spun him toward her front door. "And don't get your ass in an accident while you're at it.''

Deciding he'd take the discussion up with his mother

at a later date, he raced for the door. She was right about one thing: Elaine was very good for him.

Maybe he had something worth saving.

He tried not to drive like a maniac, but it was all he could do to use common sense. Somehow he got to the cabin without killing himself, but the storm had turned into a full-fledged, nasty blizzard. His heart dropped with he saw no lights on in the house and hoped it only meant the electricity went out. Maybe they all went to bed and forgot to leave a light on for him. That was it.

He tried the knob, but it was locked. Knowing Elaine had the keys he'd been given, he rooted around by the steps for the fake rock he'd been told also held a house key. Finally, under nearly a foot of snow, he found it and got the door unlocked.

The moment he stepped inside he knew he was alone, and he didn't need the chill from the still-lowered thermostat to do it. The place had a deserted air. His stomach tightened with fear and he ran from room to room searching for any sign that Elaine and the children had arrived ahead of him.

There was none.

ELAINE WONDERED if breaking and entering was a five-year prison term or a ten.

After walking about a half a mile, she had been about to turn the kids around for the car, realizing just how stupid she'd been to leave it. Then she'd spotted a house about a hundred feet from the road. She'd thought she found their borrowed place, but the keys Ross had given her didn't fit the lock. Knowing she was in deep trouble, she had tossed a rock through a door window and unlocked the door. At least they were out of the storm.

"I'm cold!" Ariel cried, huddling under their only quilt.

"And I'm hungry!" Jimmy added, shivering along with her.

"I'm trying to get a fire started," she said, tossing wood from a pile she'd found out back onto the living room fireplace. It was wet and she didn't think she'd get it going even if she found matches. But she'd damn well try.

Two logs fell off for every one she put on the pile. Finally, she sat back and said, "At least we all got to go to the bathroom."

"Yeah, but we couldn't flush 'cause there was no water," Jimmy said. "That's pretty icky."

"That's the owner's problem, not ours." Elaine made a silly face but the boy didn't smile.

Not only was there was no water turned on, but the thermostat didn't respond, and the house held no telephone or furniture at all. It had probably been up for sale for a long time, she surmised, since no one was even using it. She had brought the cell phone, but it still wouldn't work.

She could walk farther for help, but that would mean leaving the kids. She would *not* do that. Better to stay put and wait, now that they had decent shelter.

"I'm hungry," Ariel said. "I want my dinner."

"I want two dinners," Jimmy told her.

"I want three!"

"Four!"

Elaine tried not to panic. She'd looked in a few cabinets in the kitchen, but hadn't found much beyond a forgotten pot, pan and plate.

"Maybe Santa will bring us dinner," Ariel said.

"I don't think Santa can find us," Jimmy said, his voice cracking. "Daddy can't, either!"

Elaine turned around from her one step forward, two steps back fire building. She was about to open her mouth to allay his fears when Ariel stood up and screamed.

"I want Santa! I want Santa! I want my daddy! I want my daddy!"

"Ariel, calm down," Elaine said helplessly.

The little girl ran around in circles, paying no attention. Jimmy screamed back at her. "Shut up! Shut up! Shut up!

An inner restraint snapped inside Elaine. She roared at the top of her lungs, *"That is enough!"*

Ariel tripped in midcircle and Jimmy's jaw nearly snapped as he clamped it shut. The children looked at her wide-eyed.

"Your daddy will find us," she said sternly. "The police will find us. Santa will find you two. Maybe not right here, but your presents will be waiting for you at the cabin when we get there tomorrow. You are not forgotten. I won't let that happen. I won't let anything happen to you two. And how could your daddy not find you? That's ridiculous. He loves you so much, can't you feel it? I can. So no more screaming. No more complaining. I'm trying to get us all warm with a fire, then I'll find us something to eat after that. Somehow. Even if it's only snow. Snow's fun to eat, but we've got to melt it first. Both of you come here."

The children reluctantly got to their feet, eyeing her with caution. She brought Ariel to her and vigorously rubbed the child down from shoulders to feet, through the winter coat and leggings, then gave her a big hug. She did the same to Jimmy.

"Now you two get back under the blanket and try to sleep. As soon and I get everything set, we'll all curl up together and keep each other warm."

She helped the kids cocoon themselves up in the quilt. When they were settled, she went back to trying to pile wood for a fire. She was doing her best and knew it wasn't nearly good enough to help the kids.

Please, she thought. *Please, Ross, find us now.*

ROSS DROVE SLOWLY, hampered less by the unplowed road than by his fear that he might miss spotting Elaine's car in the early-morning light. At least the snow had finally stopped on Christmas morning, but it hadn't given him the present he wished for.

"Please," he whispered. "Just let someone find them safe and sound. That's all I ask."

He had called the police last night and the hospitals—and his mother and Elaine's parents in Las Vegas and even Burt—in his desperation to discover where Elaine and the kids were. Everyone was ready to come to him, if the trio weren't found by noon. He prayed they had holed up in some motel between the mountains and home and would arrive at the house as soon as the roads cleared, safe and sound. That was the cops' theory, although they promised to put out a county-wide alert for them. Ross waited for word, a phone call, anything, until about three in the morning when he could stand it no longer. He went out looking for them and had been out ever since.

How stupid could he have been over Elaine? His mother would tell him pretty stupid. She was damn right. Being out in the snowstorm nearly sliding off the road a million times was nothing compared to that.

He knew now that he had been trying to mold her into a cook and baby-sitter, not someone to love him and love the kids. His guardian angels had been looking out for them but he'd been too busy as Mr. Daddy Perfect Club to see what they'd provided. He wanted another chance with her, to make things right.

The sun was fully over the horizon, giving the snow a glistening blue-white glow and a promise. Ross was on some little road in God only knew what place. He couldn't imagine that Elaine had gotten herself back this far in the mountains and even farther from the nearest town.

A big, odd lump half on, half off the road caught his eye. He stopped his car and got out. Scraping off some snow revealed a car exactly like Elaine's. He wished he had her license plate memorized, although the vehicle had a New Jersey plate. This had to be her car. Fear rose up in him again that they had had a bad accident. Distraught, he shoved snow off the vehicle. It looked okay, no dents or bumps. The car doors were locked when he tried them, and the inside was deserted.

"How could she leave the car?" he asked out loud, horrified at the thought that they went wandering in the storm.

But it was clear something had happened and they had left the car. He didn't even want to think they didn't leave voluntarily. He got back in his car and tried to call the police, but static was heavy. Clearly this was a bad spot for the signals. He drove back down the road where he'd made his last call to the cops and reported the location, hoping they could tell him someone had already found them. They didn't. But they promised to come out and to keep looking.

His heart in his mouth, he tried to figure out in which direction the three could have gone. He couldn't believe they would leave the car in a snowstorm. Maybe Elaine alone, but not with two little kids...

He returned to her car, then continued forward in the direction he judged the car had been pointing before it went off the road. Logic said they would move forward in search of help rather than where they had found none yet.

He saw a house, the first he'd spotted on the road and pulled in, hoping maybe the owners would have seen or heard something of Elaine and the kids.

No cars were parked next to the house and it didn't have a garage. He almost turned back again, despairing of hope, when he noticed the broken windowpane in the front door. When he was on the front stoop, he heard voices.

He pounded on the door. "Hello? Hello!"

His heart leaped when he saw his daughter running toward him on the other side. He turned the knob, frantic to get to her, and the door opened, almost flinging him inside. He swept Ariel up in his arms and swung her around in a circle.

"Oh, God. Oh, God," he said. "You're alive. You're all right."

"Daddy! Daddy!" she shouted. "You came!"

"Daddy!"

Jimmy raced over and leg locked him, almost bowling him over. Ross lifted his son with one arm and hugged him tightly.

"You're both okay!"

"Wait till you see what we did!" Jimmy shouted in his ear.

Ross didn't care that he was deaf. He had his children again. He closed his eyes and whispered a thank-you to whoever watched over them in the night.

When he opened his eyes, Elaine stood in front of him, tears in her eyes. She looked radiant, perfect, serene and sensual. Forget what she should have done for safety's sake, he thought. In her estimable way, she had done just great.

"I love you, and I have been a fool," he said to her.

"So have I," she whispered back.

Ariel and Jimmy drew her into the embrace. Ross kissed her tenderly, eternally grateful to feel her against him once again, warm and soft. He kissed her and kissed her, tasting her richness, her uniqueness.

"You are the best Christmas present," she said finally.

"Santa didn't forget, 'Laine," Ariel said.

"No, he didn't."

They all untangled themselves and went to the living room to get their things. Ross stopped when he saw a fire, smoking more than burning in the fireplace. A pot of what looked like glue bits sat next to it. A pine branch leaned against the stone facing. It was almost falling over from the top-heavy mitten hanging from it. Several barrettes were attached and his daughter's wild hair gave him a good guess where they came from.

"We got a tree!" Ariel shouted, jumping up and down. "We made it ourselves."

"I put the mitten on it!" Jimmy shouted.

"So what, you poopy-head!" Ariel shouted back, shoving him, clearly jealous that her big brother was taking attention from her.

Ross opened his mouth, but the sudden, sharp rebuke didn't come from him.

"Ariel, that is not the way to behave!" Elaine said. "Apologize to your brother this instant."

"I'm sorry," Ariel said, looking contrite.

"Both of you calm down now," Elaine added, "or you will have to sit for five minutes on the quilt and we'll have to wait to go home."

Jimmy nodded. He looked nearly as contrite as his sister.

"Wow," Ross said, whistling. "What happened here?"

"I got a fire lit," Elaine said proudly. "After about an hour. And I found some rice and made it. It's the pits but we liked it. Right, kids?"

"I ate snow, too!" Ariel said excitedly, then toned it down. "That was good."

"But cereal is better," Jimmy announced, then ducked when Elaine playfully lunged at him.

"We were just sitting here, admiring our little Christmas tree and telling each other what gifts we already had for Christmas," she said to Ross, smiling. "I said our best gift was finding this house."

"And I said we had a fire and a tree," Jimmy said. "And some food. And we could go to the bathroom. But we can't flush."

Ross didn't ask. He didn't want to know.

"And I said we had Elaine," Ariel announced, hugging her "gift." Elaine hugged her back, then Jimmy piled on top of both of them in a free-for-all of affection.

Ross didn't even try to swallow back the lump of tears in his throat. Their easy way with each other showed another change had happened during the night.

He would get the details later. All he cared about was that his family was safe.

His mother had been absolutely right. Elaine was perfect in ways he hadn't considered. And when she'd been left to her own devices, she had cared for the children and kept them secure. He would never worry about that aspect of their lives again.

Red flashing lights filtered through the windows. The official rescuers had arrived.

Ross pulled Elaine out from under his children. He brushed her hair back from her face and smiled. "Marry me."

Elaine stared at him for a moment, her gaze searching his. He knew she would find no fear, no concern, no insecurities. "Yes."

"Merry Christmas, my love," he whispered and kissed her.

Epilogue

The reception was held at Hardware and Muffins, catered by Ruth Naomi's friends and served up by The Daddy Club. If anyone needed a miter box or a tenpenny nail, they could get a discount—for the day only.

Micah's band played everything from "Walking on Sunshine" to "Take the A Train" to "Bad Moon Rising." They were a huge hit.

"Thanks for the last song," Ross said wryly. "What was it? A warning?"

"Hey, you keep taking the plunge," Micah said, grinning at his younger brother while the band was in between sets.

"You guys are a great wedding band," Elaine said, coming up to them. "Don't change a thing."

"Don't intend to. Can I kiss the bride?"

"You already did that," Ross muttered as Micah kissed Elaine on the cheek.

"You inspired me, you know," Elaine said to Micah.

"I did?"

"He did?" Ross echoed, shocked by that news.

Elaine nodded. "You made me see that I didn't have

to be superwoman and supermom to be decent domestic material."

Micah chuckled. "I don't know where you got that from, but I'm glad it's working for you."

"Daddy, look! A real puppy!"

Ariel and Jimmy shouted with excitement as they each half carried a squirmy, red-brown bundle of short fur between them. Elaine scooped the dachshund up and presented it to Ross.

"Meet Maxine," she said. "I bought her as wedding present for the kids."

"You have got to be kidding!" Ross gasped, as the puppy licked his face. "We're going on a honeymoon. It's the worst time to have a puppy!"

"Yep. So, with my usual timing, I figured it would be good." Elaine grinned.

Maxine suddenly stopped kissing Ross on the face. The dog pressed her forehead to Ross's and looked him right in the eye from less than an inch away—then started kissing him all over again.

Ross sighed. "I think I'm in love."

"Everyone having fun?" Ruth Naomi asked, escorted by Burt who didn't seem to be giving up on her.

"We're having a blast, Mom," Ross said, handing the puppy down to his children after admonishing them that Maxine was still a baby and to be careful.

"How about a different kiss?" Elaine asked.

Ross sighed again. "If I must."

He kissed her for all he was worth, grateful she was his. Life would be chaotic, but it would be filled with love. What more could he ask for?

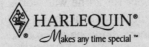

If you enjoyed what you just read,
then we've got an offer you can't resist!

Take 2 bestselling love stories FREE!

Plus get a FREE surprise gift!

HARLEQUIN®
AMERICAN ◆ ROMANCE®

Coming in January 2000—
a very special 2-in-1 story...

**Two sexy heroes, two determined heroines,
two full romances...one complete novel!**

Sophie's a stay-at-home mom.
Carla's a no-nonsense businesswoman.
Neither suspects that trading places for a week
will change their lives forever....

HIS, HERS AND THEIRS (#808)
by Debbi Rawlins
January 2000

*Join us for twice the fun, twice the romance
when two sisters-in-law trade places and fall in
love with men they wouldn't otherwise have met!
Only from Harlequin American Romance®!*

Available at your favorite retail outlet.

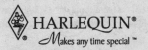

HARLEQUIN®
Makes any time special ™

COMING NEXT MONTH

Visit us at www.romance.net

CNM0100